D1395944

LUCREZIA'S SECRET

In England, Lacey's uncle, a perfumier, wants to re-create Lucrezia Borgia's own perfume. He sends his niece to Capri to obtain the secret formula. Aware of the danger that her mission might be foiled, Lacey fears that there's nobody she can trust — especially when there's a scruffy young man who seems to be stalking her. But when Scott, the helpful Texan, befriends Lacey, will she find that her suspicions about the unkempt and scarily ubiquitous Rob are all wrong?

TONI ANDERS

LUCREZIA'S SECRET

Complete and Unabridged

LINFORD
Leicester

First published in Great Britain in 2009

First Linford Edition
published 2010

British Library CIP Data

Anders, Toni.
  Lucrezia's secret. - -
  (Linford romance library)
  1. Perfumes- -Formulae- -Fiction. 2. Capri
  (Italy)- -Fiction. 3. Romantic suspense novels.
  4. Large type books.
  I. Title II. Series
  823.9'2–dc22

  ISBN 978–1–44480–146–0

Published by
F. A. Thorpe (Publishing)
Anstey, Leicestershire

Set by Words & Graphics Ltd.
Anstey, Leicestershire
Printed and bound in Great Britain by
T. J. International Ltd., Padstow, Cornwall

This book is printed on acid-free paper

1

'But Uncle Max, there are professional couriers who can do this sort of thing for you.' Lacey looked at the old man in exasperation. She had been arguing with him for the past hour.

Uncle Max stuck out his bottom lip, a gesture she well remembered from her childhood. She knew it meant that no matter how hard she argued, he would have his own way.

'Let me explain to you again,' he said, refilling her wine glass. 'The formula for the perfume is priceless. There are people who would do anything — anything — to get hold of it. No one would suspect a pretty young lady travelling on holiday to a romantic island like Capri. A professional courier would stick out like the proverbial sore thumb.'

Lacey sipped her wine. 'How do

these people know about the formula?'

'They've found out — somehow. Perhaps Claudia Capua let the secret escape. She was warned to say nothing, but you know Italian women! They chatter. They confide in people. Anyway, someone has found out about it. They've made approaches to me and to Giovanni.'

'Approaches. Do you mean threats?'

'Not yet. At the moment it's just offers of money. When they realise we won't sell, they'll threaten — or steal.'

'That doesn't make me feel very safe.'

Lacey finished her wine, but put her hand over the top of her glass as her uncle reached for the bottle.

'You'll be safe enough,' he said. 'They don't know about you. We haven't met for twenty years and I set up this meeting very carefully.' He looked around the hotel room.

Lacey sat and thought. She was on holiday from her job as a language teacher at a small private school, so she really had nothing planned for the next six weeks. And Uncle Max had promised to pay all expenses for a holiday to Sorrento and Capri. So why did she hesitate?

'Tell me again, from the very beginning, what you want me to do and what this is all about,' she said.

Uncle Max smiled as if he'd already got his own way.

'Giovanni Estrelli, my friend on Capri, discovered the formula for the favourite perfume of Lucrezia Borgia, the beautiful daughter of Pope Alexander the sixth who lived in the fifteenth century.'

'Who was also a famous poisoner,' Lacey said.

'That has never been proved conclusively,' he said dismissively, 'and has no bearing on this. The point is, she was famous and beautiful and had the best of everything. So a perfume created for her would be exquisite.'

'How did your friend discover it?'

'He is a chemist and a writer. He

3

researches obscure old books and manuscripts. He came across references to the perfume and worked on them until he was sure he had the formula.'

'So where does Claudia Capua come into the story?'

'She is a Lucrezia of the twenty-first century,' he said. He caught her eye. 'But not, of course, a poisoner. She is famous and beautiful and expects the absolute best of everything.'

'She's getting married in a few months,' said Lacey, 'or so I've read in all the upmarket magazines.'

'Exactly. And for her wedding, she wants to wear Lucrezia's perfume.'

'So all this is because a famous Italian film star wants an exclusive perfume?'

'And will pay well for it,' he nodded. 'After the wedding, her husband, a wealthy business man, intends to market it which, of course, will make a great deal of money. So secrecy is essential. The formula mustn't fall into the hands of the wrong people. It would not be safe to send it by post, it must be collected in person and delivered to me in London.'

'Where you will create it?'

'Precisely. I will create this exclusive perfume right here in my own personal laboratory where I have everything I need.' Uncle Max was a famous perfumier and this creation would be a feather in his cap as well as a fortune in his pocket.

'And you really think I can collect this formula from Giovanni and bring it safely back to London?'

'I know you can. You are so like your mother. My dear sister was fearless. If she set her mind to something, no matter how difficult, she would achieve it.'

Lacey smiled gently. She barely remembered her mother, who had died when she was small. But she had heard many stories of her exploits in the mountains of Kashmir from where she had fallen to her death.

'I don't think I can match up to her,'

she said, 'but if you think I can do what you want, I'll try.'

Uncle Max got up from his chair and came over to her, a smile on his face.

'My dear girl,' he said, and lifting her to her feet, enveloped her in a bear hug. 'You don't know what this means. Thank you, thank you.'

He rang a bell beside the door and sat down again, still beaming. A few minutes later, the door opened to reveal a smartly dressed waiter pushing a trolley on which was laid a sumptuous supper.

'You can't leave until it is dark,' said her uncle, tucking a large napkin beneath his chin. 'So we'll eat now and then after supper I'll get you all your instructions and tickets.'

★ ★ ★

For the next hour, they chatted of her school and his famous clients while Lacey ate far too much of the creamed chicken and asparagus and then tiny

6

fruit fools and meringue. Replete, at last, she sat back in her chair.

'That was superb,' she sighed.

'Wasn't it?' he agreed. 'The chef here really is in a class of his own. Now,' he reached across to a small table at his side and picked up a brown envelope. 'If these dates don't suit, they can be altered, but you did say that you were free for the next few weeks.'

She nodded. He took a pile of tickets and money from the envelope.

'Your plane ticket to Capodichino Airport at Naples on the twenty-first. A hotel booking for the San Gennaro Hotel in Sorrento for a week and a return ticket for the twenty-eighth. That should give you plenty of time. And of course, your euros. I think you'll find I have been generous.' He gave her a smile.

'These dates, Uncle . . . ' She looked up at him questioningly. 'How did you know I would agree to do this?'

'I counted on your spirit of adventure, my dear. I thought the story would appeal to you that way.'

She took the envelope and stowed it away in her bag.

'Giovanni's name and address are in the envelope,' he said, 'but you will also need a password.'

'A password?' Lacey laughed. 'Very cloak and dagger!'

'But very essential. The password is Maria Elena.'

'Maria Elena. A girl's name?'

'You will say to Giovanni, 'You and Max were both in love with Maria Elena'.'

'And were you?'

'In love with Maria Elena? Yes. She was Giovanni's cousin. I met her at his house when we were students.'

'And she had to choose between you?'

'No. She was in love with someone else. She hardly knew we existed. But no one else would know this story so Giovanni will know you have come from me.'

'When did you last see Giovanni?'

'Just over a year ago. We met in Paris

after he phoned to tell me he had something secret and exciting to discuss. The formula wasn't ready then but it was nearly complete and we made plans. I said I would send a messenger to collect it when he gave the signal.'

'Why don't you go yourself?'

'I don't find walking very easy nowadays. I don't travel far. Paris was easy. I went on the Eurostar. But Sorrento and Capri — aeroplanes, cars, ferries — no, I don't think so.'

'So you thought of me?'

'Yes. Although we haven't met for years because you've lived in America, your letters have kept me in touch with you. I was so pleased when you returned to this country and began to work here. I knew I'd see more of you again.'

'I'd planned to come and see you as soon as I got a holiday,' Lacey said, 'but your letter arrived before I could contact you. I was intrigued with the secrecy of the meeting.' She gestured round the hotel sitting room.

'When this is over, you must come and stay in my house in London,' said her uncle enthusiastically. 'We'll plan some outings, theatres, dinners, trips on the river. Would you like that?'

'Oh yes, I don't know London at all.'

'Good. But for the time being, we mustn't be seen together. Now, we must get you out of here. If I was followed to this hotel, they could be watching and waiting. We must leave separately.'

Lacey collected her coat and bag and stood up.

'At the end of the corridor is a door marked Private,' said Uncle Max. 'Once you are certain that no one is around, slip through the door and down three flights of stairs. You will come out in the laundry of the hotel. There should be no one in there at this time of day. I've already arranged for the door into the yard to be left open. From there, it is only a few steps to the right and you will be in the main road. There are plenty of taxis. You should have no difficulty in finding one. Are you happy about this?'

'My adventure begins,' smiled Lacey. 'But what about you?'

'Don't worry about me. I might stay here for a day or two. By then, they'll think I've left and that they missed me.' He put his hand on her shoulder and kissed her on both cheeks.

'Goodbye, my dear girl. When you return on the twenty-eighth come back to this hotel where I will be waiting for you. I have every confidence in you and I simply know you will be successful and bring back what I want. Have a wonderful holiday while you do!' He went to the door, stuck his head out and took a quick look up and down the corridor. Still standing in the doorway he beckoned to Lacey. Still slightly amused at her uncle's cloak-and-dagger antics, she slipped past him and he quickly closed the door behind her.

* * *

Lacey hurried silently along the thick carpet of the corridor to the door marked Private. It opened silently and she went through. She closed it, checking that no one had appeared in the corridor behind her and began to descend the flight of bare wooden stairs.

She counted three flights and found herself facing a glass panel in a heavy door. The glass was worn but she could see through it into the laundry, which certainly seemed to be deserted.

She could feel her heart beating rapidly as she quickly opened the door. Small working lights shone eerily round the large room. Huge washing machines waited against the walls. She could hear mysterious rumbles and clicks. It was decidedly spooky, she thought.

In the opposite wall was a large door and set within it, a smaller one. She crossed hastily to this, slipped through and thankfully breathed the night air. Above her, a sliver of moon appeared and vanished between thick clouds. It was dark, but a street-lamp opposite gave a welcome light.

A quick glance up and down the alley showed it to be deserted. She turned right as instructed and was soon in the evening bustle of the main road.

Uncle Max was right. There were plenty of taxis. Hailing one, she climbed in and settled back into the corner of the seat with a sigh of relief.

Thinking back over the last few hours, she felt faintly ridiculous. What was she, Lacey Kent, doing pretending to be a female James Bond?

Unlike her mother, she didn't seek danger. She'd travelled a great deal but always in safety and under the protection of her father. This time she would be on her own with no one to help her.

She looked out of the window at the people hurrying home from work or to their evening entertainment. They all seemed to know where they were going. They all had a purpose.

What was her purpose for the next six weeks, until school began again? She knew few people in England. Apart from Uncle Max she had no relations left, no one who would be glad to see her.

Perhaps she should develop a sense of adventure; be like her mother and not fear danger? It was a new idea. Lacey Kent, special agent, she thought to herself with a giggle.

The driver turned into her road. 'The house next to the large tree,' she directed, and he drew to a halt.

A few minutes later she was back in her own flat, kicking off her shoes, switching on her coffee percolator and the gas fire and flinging herself on to the couch in front of the fire. She lay back and closed her eyes. What would her father be doing now in his log cabin in the Adirondacks? She smiled. Probably gazing in horror at the dirty dishes and unmade bed waiting for his attention. He'd never been domesticated. There was no need for him to learn because she'd always been with him.

But she'd drawn the line at log cabins in the mountains. And she had to admit, she'd had enough of America. She wanted to return to her roots, even if they were shallow ones.

On the death of her mother when she was six, she'd been taken in by an adoring grandmother. Her father was a diplomat travelling the world and this lifestyle was considered too unsettling for a child. Uncle Max was the only other male figure in her life and she saw him only occasionally.

But her life changed dramatically within a few months when her grandmother suffered a stroke that left her unable to care for a young child, and to the sorrow of both of them, they had to part.

Reluctantly at first, her father decided she had better live with him. The discovery of the perfect nanny made him realise that, spared the day to day care of a little girl, she could be a source of delight, a small person who could be helped and guided and who would repay him with devotion.

They lived very happily for the next twenty years in several different countries, but mostly in America, her father's favourite. Lacey learned how to mix with all sorts of people, to ride and ski and sail a boat, and how to make herself understood in several languages.

All this fitted her for life as the wife of a diplomat, but so far, no serious romance had entered her life.

She seldom thought about her future, but when she did, she felt a vague feeling that she didn't want a gilded existence. She wanted to build a worthwhile life with a man who valued her help. She didn't want everything handed to her on a plate. It would be more interesting to work and fight for it.

She could never discuss this with her father. He imagined they would stay together forever. In his fond but selfish view, she would always be with him. So when, on his retirement, he announced his intention of moving to a mountain resort to live in what Lacey mischievously referred to as a log cabin, he was astonished when she refused to go with him.

'But what will you do?' he'd asked.

'What will I do if I come with you?' she'd retorted. 'I'm not quite ready to retire at twenty-seven. I can't spend my life playing bowls and card games.'

For a few days there'd been a frostiness between them, then he'd realised the unfairness of the situation.

Finally, after a lot of discussion, he'd agreed to her applying for the job at the school in England and had even been genuinely pleased for her when she'd got it. She'd set off for England and he'd settled himself in the mountains where he seemed blissfully happy.

The letter from Uncle Max had come out of the blue. They'd corresponded occasionally, but she hadn't heard from him for some time. Now he wrote suggesting the meeting in London, giving her careful directions and emphasising the need for complete secrecy. Intrigued, she'd written to agree to his request.

The coffee percolator began to

bubble frantically and she stood up to pour herself a cup. Catching sight of herself in the mirror, a thought struck her. Clothes. Most of her summer clothes were back at her flat near the school. She'd brought only a few to London.

The flat she was in now belonged to the sister of a fellow teacher who was on holiday in Spain. She'd lent it to Lacey for two weeks while she decided what to do with her holiday. There was no time to collect her clothes; she'd need a shopping expedition tomorrow.

She sat down with a pen and paper and began to make a list. Capri was in a very hot part of Italy — she'd need sun dresses, shorts and lots of sun block cream. For the next half hour she thought and wrote her list, happily planning her wardrobe. She had two days before her flight — that ought to be more than enough time for shopping.

★   ★   ★

The ring of the telephone made her jump. It must be for the owner of the flat; because few people knew she was here.

'Hello.' Her tone was impersonal.

'Lacey. Good. You're back.' Of course, Uncle Max.

'I've been back some time.'

'No problems?'

'No.' She laughed. 'No watchers in the shadows.'

'Lacey. I hope you'll treat this whole affair seriously. I said there is little danger to you, but do please be careful. Don't drop your guard. I shall feel happier when you are back.'

'With the formula.'

'Of course, with the formula. But the main thing is for you to get back home safely, my dear,' he said, concerned.

'Don't worry, Uncle Max, I shall be very careful. I'll take no chances.'

'Good girl. I won't contact you again. If you need me, my number is in the envelope. Good luck, my dear.'

Lacey replaced the telephone feeling

19

suddenly very tired. It had been an eventful evening. Time for bed.

But before going into her bedroom she went to her bookcase and selected an encyclopedia. Turning to the second section, she ran her finger down the page.

BORGIA. Cesare. Son of Pope Alexander VI.

BORGIA. Lucrezia. b. 1480. Sister of Cesare. Married at twelve, thirteen and again at eighteen.

Lacey made a face. She returned to the page.

In 1501, she read, Lucrezia was found a fourth husband.

For which wedding was the coveted perfume created, Lacey wondered? She studied the portrait. Lucrezia was certainly beautiful — at least as lovely as the modern young woman who wanted her exclusive perfume for her own wedding.

She returned the book to the shelf and went into the bedroom to get herself ready for bed. Sleep was a long time coming and when she finally managed to drift off, she dreamt that she was chasing Lucrezia Borgia down a dark alley with a bundle of washing under her arm.

2

In the taxi to the airport, dressed in a new pale blue linen trouser suit, Lacey patted her suitcase with satisfaction. It contained the collection of holiday wear she'd spent the day before accumulating. She felt prepared for anything.

The taxi stopped in front of the entrance to the airport. She climbed out, secured a trolley, loaded up and pushed it slowly through the crowds of excited holiday makers towards the British Airways desk.

At the desk, an untidy young man was just finishing his transaction. He was tall and a worn denim jacket fitted his broad shoulders like a second skin. He turned away and his eyes met Lacey's. He gave her a keen and lingering glance and she felt herself blushing.

When she'd finished checking in, she

turned to see him, partly concealed, watching her from behind a pillar. His hair was combed flat against his head and his chin bristled with scruffy designer stubble.

His one redeeming feature was a pair of startlingly blue eyes, which quickly flicked away when he realised that she had noticed him watching her.

Lacey breathed deeply to calm herself. To the side, she saw the sign to the ladies room. He could hardly follow her there. Forcing herself to walk naturally, she made her way up the short corridor.

In the mirror she saw the door behind her open and a girl of about her own age came in. The girl went to the far end of the long mirror and began to pull a comb through her short, curly brown hair. Her eyes met Lacey's and she hastily looked away without the trace of a smile. She was a stranger but Lacey had the feeling that there was something familiar about her.

She applied a faint, unnecessary dusting of powder to the end of her nose.

There were several chatting girls at the mirror. Lacey began to breathe naturally.

Why should she imagine he was watching her?

The entrance hall was packed with people. He had to look somewhere. If she was going to imagine crooks everywhere when she hadn't even reached Italy, she would have an uncomfortable time.

As Uncle Max had said, who would suspect a young girl, obviously going on a summer holiday, of being a secret courier? No one had seen her leave the hotel two nights ago, of that she was absolutely certain, and there was nothing to connect her to Uncle Max.

She picked up her travel case and shoulder bag, took a steadying breath and left the ladies room. In the entrance hall, there was no sign of the young man. She glanced at her watch. She had nearly two hours to fill. She headed for the restaurant, suddenly aware that she'd had no breakfast and was beginning to feel decidedly hungry.

The restaurant was crowded but she found a small table in a corner. She'd chosen coffee and croissants which were surprisingly fresh. And they actually had cherry jam, her favourite. She took a book from her bag, propped it against the coffee pot and began to enjoy her breakfast.

'Excuse me, ma'am. Would you mind very much if I shared your table? I won't take up much room.'

Startled, Lacey looked up into a pair of huge brown eyes in a tanned face. The man was tall and heavily built and looked as if he would take up a lot of room, but the Texan accent was reassuring to someone who had spent so long in America, and without thinking, Lacey nodded and moved her book to the side. She left it on the table; she didn't want it to seem as if she intended to talk to him. But she had reckoned without the chattiness of the American abroad.

'You goin' on holiday, ma'am?' he began.

She gave him a little smile. 'Yes,' and

25

returned to her book.

'Me too. I'm going to see a little bit of Italy and France before I go home to the good old US of A.'

He wanted to chat. She gave in. 'You've been on holiday in Britain?'

'Working. Visiting lecturer at the City College in London. Been here since Christmas.' He was rapidly demolishing a large plate of bacon and eggs.

'My name's Scott Marner by the way.' He put out a large hand which enveloped Lacey's small one.

'Lacey Kent,' she said. 'I'm a language teacher.'

'Well, we're in the same line of business,' he smiled.

Somehow she found herself telling him about the places she knew in America and about her father's home in the Adirondacks.

The man was a lecturer. What could be more respectable? But she nevertheless retained enough caution not to mention Uncle Max.

'Can I get you another coffee — or

something stronger? Do you need a drink to give you Dutch courage?'

'No thank you. I'm not afraid of flying. I've done too much of it.'

'You're braver than me,' he admitted. 'I think I'll just get a Bourbon. Excuse me. Oh, would you keep an eye on my bags?'

She watched his retreating back and looked at the pile of bags he had left in her care. She really would have to extricate herself from this man as soon as she possibly could; she really couldn't afford to have a travelling companion.

There was a queue at the bar and it was quite a while before he returned carrying a glass and wearing a sheepish expression.

'Silly, isn't it,' he said as he sat down. 'I've flown enough to be used to it but at the eleventh hour I get butterflies. Hey, is anything wrong?'

Lacey had glanced across the restaurant and found the scruffy young man again watching her from a seat near the door. Her sharp intake of breath had been noticed by her companion.

'Is anything wrong?' he asked again.

'I'm probably being silly but I think I may be being stalked,' she said anxiously. 'Watched, anyway.'

'Who . . . ' he began, starting to turn in his seat.

'No.' She held her hand out to stop him. 'Don't turn round. It's a young man and I've seen him watching me on two occasions downstairs, and now he's here and he's watching me again.'

'Well I can't say I'm surprised,' said the Texan gallantly. 'You're most definitely worth watching.'

'Please,' she protested.

'I'm sorry. You do look worried. But is there any reason why he should be watching you or following you?'

Lacey felt she daren't confide in this stranger. How could she know if anyone was what he seemed?

'No, of course not. The idea is simply ridiculous. I'm not even remotely famous or wealthy. Why should he want to follow me?' She wished she'd said nothing about the young man.

Scott Marner sipped his drink thoughtfully. 'What about this idea,' he said, at last. 'Why don't we travel together? Then he can't bother you. You are going to Naples, aren't you?'

'Oh no.' Lacey's protest was instant. 'I mean,' she was aware it sounded rude, 'Yes, I am going to Naples but I prefer to travel alone. I like to read.' She smiled apologetically, 'Besides, we might not be travelling in the same class. Are you travelling business class?' She had a feeling he wasn't and silently blessed Uncle Max's generosity.

He grinned. 'No. But I could upgrade.'

'Please, don't. I'll be all right, really.'

'Well, he won't be travelling business class, that's for sure,' said the Texan.

Lacey looked at the young man under her lashes and agreed. Then a thought struck her. If he was going to Naples and travelling business class, then he probably was stalking her. She just stopped herself confiding this in Scott. He might insist on upgrading to travel with her and she must shake him off somehow. It would be too much of a strain having to watch everything she said, however comforting his presence might be.

The young man had gone up to the counter and stood with his back towards her. Now was her chance, she thought. She stood up.

'I'll slip out now while he's not looking this way,' she said quickly. 'I still need to get myself another book and some mints. I'll see you around, I expect.'

Before he could insist on going with her, she had hurried from the restaurant and down to the mall of shops. She dived into the bookshop and concealed herself behind a wall of paperbacks, hoping that neither of them would find her.

* * *

Before too long, her flight was called. She made her way to the gate and joined the queue. There was no sign of

Scott or the young man. She breathed a sigh of relief. She'd soon be tucked away in business class and could forget them for a few hours.

A smiling check-in girl held out a hand for her boarding pass and passport and turned to speak to a colleague. Lacey glanced back over her shoulder. Still no sign of them. Of course, the young man might be travelling to another part of Italy, not Naples. She shuffled her feet impatiently as she waited for the passport to be returned to her.

At last she set off down the tunnel and into the plane. Another paintbox-bright stewardess welcomed her and yet another indicated where she should sit.

The plane was half empty and she had plenty of room to spread herself and her belongings over two seats. It was not long before they were moving towards the end of the runway. This was the moment Lacey always feared. She glanced around. The businessmen who were her travelling companions were already engrossed in files and sheaves of papers. No fears there, she thought.

The surge of power as the engines prepared to move the huge machine down the runway pushed her back into her seat. Then they were off the ground safely and climbing towards the blue sky. The plane levelled out and as the engine roar subsided a little, Lacey relaxed. She closed her eyes and for the next half hour was conscious only of the low droning of the engine and the occasional rustle of papers in the cabin.

She let her thoughts wander pleasurably over her shopping trip of the previous day. The aquamarine one piece bathing costume with a matching pareo was especially flattering. Of course, Sorrento had no beach, so she'd have to go further afield. She might hire a car.

The plane suddenly tilted to the right then steadied itself again, but the jolt caused a shiny magazine on her lap to slide into the aisle. She bent to retrieve it and as she straightened up she glanced across the aisle. From a seat a few rows back, the scruffy man was watching her.

Lacey stiffened. So he was stalking her! Why hadn't she accepted Scott's offer to accompany her? What could she do now? She was safe while she was on the plane, but what about when they landed? How could she avoid him?

Thoughts whirled furiously round her head. She'd planned to take a train from the airport to Sorrento, but now she had to revise her plans; she would be too vulnerable on a train.

It would be best to hire a car and driver. That way, she would not be travelling alone. On landing, she had only to get herself to the hire car desk and she would be safe. He could hardly try to approach her in such a public place.

But what if he followed her to the hotel? It was expensive but he was obviously able to spend money other-wise he would not have turned up in business class. His employers must have told him to do what was necessary to follow her. By now, Lacey was convinced he was in the pay of the people who wanted the formula.

She began to plan carefully. On arrival at the hotel, she would conceal herself somewhere in the foyer and watch the door — for hours, if necessary. If he came in, she'd leave the hotel and find somewhere else to stay.

If there was no sign of him after a few hours, she could assume he didn't know where she was staying and would have to go and search for her. Then she could claim her room.

Feeling slightly better, she leaned back in her seat and closed her eyes again. Then she sat up. Scott! She'd forgotten him. Would it be a good idea to look for him at the airport and travel with him to Sorrento? The thought of his large presence was reassuring but she hesitated. If he believed she was being followed, he might insist on contacting the police. That would mean delays and explanations. No, she was better on her own.

She gestured to the stewardess and ordered a small brandy. Sipping it, she felt her courage and common sense returning.

What if she was completely wrong? What if the man had no interest in her at all? He might be a wealthy man who preferred to go round looking like a scruff. Perhaps he, too, was trying to put off stalkers.

Perhaps he was a famous film star or a pop singer travelling in disguise. She smiled to herself and realised she was feeling better. It must be the brandy.

The sign came on instructing passengers to fasten their seatbelts. Not long now. She gathered together her travelling case, her magazines and her handbag and prepared for the descent.

As soon as the signal was given she would be off the plane at the head of the queue. She braced herself for the moment when the plane would come to a stop.

Oh no! She'd forgotten the luggage carrousel. She'd have to wait there until her suitcase arrived. He had only to stand there and wait for her. All her fears returned. She sandwiched herself between two portly Italian businessmen and managed to reach the luggage carrousel partly concealed by them. There was no sign of her stalker.

At last her case sailed through the gap. She snatched it up quickly and swung it off the carrousel.

She reached the car hire desk in safety and made her request. The desk clerk picked up his telephone.

Lacey glanced nervously towards the arrivals door where people continued to stream through. Hurry up, she urged the clerk, silently. Please hurry!

'Your car will be at the front in three minutes,' he said, as if he heard her plea.

She thanked him and pushed her way through the crowds of people and luggage and trolleys to the front of the airport.

A gleaming black car drew up. The chauffeur checked her name, opened the rear door for her and placed her suitcase on the seat beside her.

In a few seconds they were off.

The airport was close to the city and they were soon dodging through heavy traffic. Lacey was glad she'd decided against hiring a car and driving herself.

They sped through the centre of Naples passing elegant hotels, churches with impressive architecture and grand buildings housing museums and art galleries. The roads were lined with inviting shops and cafes and there were squares with fountains and flowers and intriguing alleyways.

Lacey longed to stop. She decided to come back to the city on the train and explore on her own. If I can throw off that wretched man, she thought.

Leaving the city centre behind, they entered an area of poor apartment blocks with washing and birdcages, and even bicycles on their balconies. The buildings were so crowded together that the narrow streets looked dark and gloomy. Lacey had read that over two million people lived in Naples. They could hardly all live in the city in beautiful buildings, she thought.

She felt sorry for the inhabitants of this ugly sprawl. To live near so much beauty and have such little share in it.

The depressing outskirts of Naples went on for miles. Lacey gazed through the windows, unseeing. Her mind had switched to the girl at London airport. Had she imagined her? She had stared at Lacey in the mirror for only a few minutes but there was something strange about her. Somehow, Lacey had felt as if she'd been looking at herself. Yet they were not identical. Was she a doppelganger, the double everyone is supposed to have? It was creepy.

Suddenly, Lacey became aware that the Naples sprawl was behind them and she was looking down at glowing azure water — the famous Bay of Naples.

The road twisted and turned in a terrifying way but she barely even noticed it at all. The sea view was entrancing; silver sparkles on the waves, stately white cruise ships, tiny boats buzzing to and fro and, looming over all, the impressive bulk of Mount Vesuvius.

The driver gazed impassively through the windscreen, controlling the car with skill as he passed vehicles coming towards them with only a few centimetres to spare. Lacey glanced nervously towards the low wall which edged the road on the seaward side. There was no way it would stop a car that swerved too close from hurtling from the cliff top into the sea far below.

To take her mind off the thought, she looked through the windows on the other side. The houses were quite small, but each had a garden ablaze with flowers and plants grew everywhere, despite the searing heat.

As well as flowers, there were orange and lemon trees heavy with fruit; olive trees with nets looped up ready to catch the fruit as it fell and vines trained across pergolas. These provided much needed shade in the little gardens where groups of tables and chairs were squeezed into even the smallest of spaces.

The car shot through several small towns. Signs were everywhere — shop signs, cafe and restaurant signs, as well as every type of police and traffic sign.

As well as cars, scooters swarmed everywhere. Young men drove alone, or with girlfriends draped over them; families with small children standing between the drivers' legs, or babies in the arms of the pillion riders; even, to Lacey's amazement, a little dog riding behind its master balancing on the rear seat as the scooter swerved between cars and buses. She tried to imagine a British policeman faced with these sights.

At last they drove through a much larger town, swept up to a huge pink hotel with a grand flight of steps at the front, and stopped. The driver looked at her over his shoulder, and smiled.

'San Gennaro Hotel, Sorrento.'

Lacey looked out of the back window. There were so many cars. How could she tell if one had followed her?

But she must hurry. She took out her purse.

'How much — er, quanto?'

He smiled and held up his fingers. Lacey counted out the unfamiliar euros. The driver opened her door and reached for her case, but she shook her head.

'No thank you, I can manage.' I can be up those steps faster than him, she thought and a few minutes later was entering the swing doors.

The foyer was large and cool after the intense heat of the street. Huge pillars stood at intervals round the edge, partly concealing deep sofas. With a quick look round, Lacey chose a pillar which had the added advantage of a large leafy plant just behind it, and sank on to the sofa. She had a good view of the door and taking out a magazine to conceal her face, settled down to wait.

For the next hour, there was a constant procession of people in and out of the hotel. Lacey was desperately thirsty but daren't leave her hiding place. She was just about to try and attract the attention of a passing waiter, when a figure in scruffy jeans and a denim jacket came through the swing doors. She shrank back behind her magazine. It was her stalker.

3

He must have followed me. How else would he know I was here? Sorrento is full of hotels. How did he know I was in this one? Lacey's mind was a whirl. She'd been watching the hotel door in case he turned up, but she didn't really think he would. She'd almost convinced herself that her imagination was working overtime. But he was here! Now what should she do?

From behind her magazine, she watched him approach the reception desk. If he was just asking about her, he'd leave when they said she had not turned up. Or would he also sit in the foyer and wait?

How had he managed to learn her name or why she was here? He must be part of the gang, working alone. He'd summon others when he caught her. She began to feel frantic.

But no, he was writing something and the receptionist was handing him a key and pointing to the lift.

As the lift door closed behind him, Lacey lowered her magazine and sat up. If she waited ten minutes more, she could check in and reach her room in safety. But then what? Was she to spend a week holed up in her room? This was supposed to be a holiday. And how could she get to Giovanni on Capri if she couldn't leave the hotel?

There was only one answer. Leave the hotel now. Don't stay here. Find another hotel. Willing herself to keep calm, she picked up her cases and bag and made her way to the reception desk, casting a fearful glance at the lift as she passed. What if he left his luggage in his room and came straight back down?

The clerk spoke excellent English. Lacey made up a story about having met a friend with a villa who had invited her to stay.

'So I'm afraid I'll have to cancel my

reservation,' she apologised.

'That is no problem,' smiled the clerk. 'Sorrento is full of visitors. We shall have no problem re-letting your room.'

Thanking him, Lacey hurried out of the hotel and down the steps. She was in a little square of cafés and palm trees. Though very thirsty, she decided to move just a little further away.

Her suitcase was not too heavy. She set off down a narrow cobbled street and into another small square. On the far side, tables and chairs were laid out invitingly under green canvas awnings. The café looked cool and secluded. She was soon tucked away at a corner table with a long fruit drink in front of her.

Gradually, the tension began to leave her. She sat back in her chair and observed the people at nearby tables. There were young couples, slim, tanned, engrossed in each other; family groups with small children; elegant older ladies, beautifully dressed, their dark hair shining with red highlights.

The sun was high in the blue,

cloudless sky. She was glad of the shelter of the awning. She finished her drink and signalled to the waiter for another. She felt too relaxed to leave the safety of the cafe and set off to find another hotel. But she must do so soon. The hotel clerk had said that Sorrento was full. What if she couldn't find another room?

She put her head back and closed her eyes, trying not to panic. A few minutes later a shadow fell across her face and as her eyes flickered open, she heard a familiar American voice.

'Well Miss Kent! What are you doing here?' He looked at the bags piled near her. 'And with your luggage, too. Are you on the way to your hotel? There's not a problem, is there?'

All her fears came to the surface. She felt ashamed of herself. Her mother would have dealt with problems on her own, but Lacey felt such an overwhelming feeling of relief at hearing a friendly, masculine voice. Scott was so large, so capable-looking. He would help her.

The American slid into the seat opposite. He put a large hand over her small one. 'Let me help. I know you have a problem.'

'I was right,' she said. 'He was following me. I reached my hotel safely, but I decided to wait in the foyer, hidden in a corner, and that's when I saw him come in and go up to his room.'

'Well?'

'It was the San Gennaro, one of the most expensive hotels in Sorrento. It really didn't seem his sort of place.' He smiled and she hurried on, 'I'm not being snobbish, it's just that something doesn't seem right.'

Then a worrying thought struck her. She'd told the American she was going to Naples but she'd said nothing about Sorrento. How had he found her? Was he a stalker? She drew back in alarm.

He noticed the change in her expression. 'Hey, anything wrong?'

'Well . . . how did you know I'd be in Sorrento?'

He burst out laughing. 'D'you think

I'm a stalker too?' He reached down and fingered a luggage label. 'San Gennaro Hotel, Sorrento,' he read out. 'I noticed it at the airport.'

She relaxed. 'Of course. Anyone could have read it.'

'But you've cancelled your booking there?'

'Yes. I can't have a relaxing holiday if I'm constantly worrying where he is and what he's doing. Even if I'm wrong about him, I'm going to find another hotel.'

Scott called the waiter and ordered a cold drink. He raised an inquiring eyebrow at her but she shook her head.

'I've had two, thank you.'

His beer arrived immediately and he drank half of it in one go. 'That's better. It's quite a bit different here from England, isn't it? There's hot and hot, and this certainly is hot!' He was cheerful and relaxed and watching him, Lacey felt herself relaxing too.

'Now,' he said. 'Have you another hotel in mind?'

'Well, no. I was going to walk around and see what I could find. Somewhere quiet and secluded where I could come and go without being noticed. I want to get about and see the area.' She was careful not to mention Capri.

'Time's getting on and the town is very crowded,' he pointed out. 'Do you really want to walk about in this heat with suitcases?'

She looked at him doubtfully. He finished his beer.

'This is just an idea,' he said. 'I'm staying at a villa quite near with a friend and his niece. Why don't you come there with me, just for tonight, and we'll 'phone around and find you a hotel for tomorrow? Then I'll bring you back in the morning and you can carry on with your holiday.'

She sat biting her lip. Would it be safe? What did she really know about this large American other than what he had told her? And that could be a lie.

She could telephone Uncle Max and say where she was going but the address might be false. Uncle Max would immediately be suspicious. But he hadn't met Scott. She looked across at the open, tanned face and the smile as he looked at her quizzically under heavy brows. She was suddenly sure she could trust him.

'I can see all the questions going round and round in your head,' he said, teasingly. 'If you're worried about being at the villa with two men, his niece is there, as I've said. And it will only be for one night.'

She stood up. 'Thank you. I accept. But I must come back tomorrow.'

Scott lifted her case as easily as if it weighed nothing, put a hand lightly round her waist and shepherded her across the square.

'My car is up here. Just a short walk.'

★   ★   ★

The car was small but comfortable. In a few minutes they had merged into the swift flowing traffic and Scott was weaving skillfully through the narrow streets and out of the town.

'We'll be there in twenty minutes,' he said. 'The villa is on the cliff top with wonderful sea views.'

'Won't it be hugely inconvenient for your friend if I turn up with you unannounced?' she asked.

He gave her a strange smile. 'Don't worry, they'll be delighted to see you.'

They were re-tracing the route down which Lacey had come in her hired car, but soon turned off and began to climb higher along flower-edged narrow roads overhung with scrubby pines and ancient, gnarled olive trees, and with the sparkling azure sea on her left.

She wound down the window and breathed the pine-rich air.

He glanced across at her and nodded in agreement. 'Wonderful, isn't it? Worth coming all this way just for the air.'

'Sorrento smells of lemons,' she said.

'The whole Bay of Naples smells of

lemons,' he answered. 'They grow everywhere and are used for everything — soap, perfume, sweets. There is even a speciality drink called limoncello. There are even a number of shops which sell only lemon products.'

'Have you been here many times?'

'Mm. Several. It's one of my favourite parts of Italy. And you?'

'It's my first visit,' she said.

'What made you choose it for a holiday?' The question was natural but it still served to put her instantly on her guard. 'I think someone told me about it,' she said, trying to be casual and vague.

They drove for a while in silence then began to descend towards the sea. The gates of a small villa built on the edge of the cliff, came in sight.

'What a remote place for a house,' she said.

'Remote in the old days. Now everyone has a car and there are several small villages not far away.' He stopped the car, got out and opened the gates. Then he drove forward, got out again and locked the gates behind them.

Lacey looked back uneasily at the gates as they drove up the drive. If Scott noticed, he gave no sign. He pulled up in front of a heavy, iron-studded door. It opened immediately and a stocky, swarthy-skinned man came out. He looked at Lacey as she climbed from the car but said nothing.

How strange, she thought. Doesn't he think it odd that his friend has arrived with an unknown woman.

Scott noticed the look on her face. He nodded towards the man. 'Gino,' he said. 'He's the general factotum.'

So Gino wasn't Scott's friend. He must be inside. Leaving Gino to deal with the luggage, the American led the way into a stone hall, invitingly cool after the temperature outside.

'Come along. Let's find your host.'

Lacey followed him into a large salon overlooking the sea. She didn't know what sort of man she expected to see, but it certainly wasn't the tiny wizened figure who waited for them on a chaise longue in the window.

He was fully dressed, but despite the warmth of the day, wrapped in a brightly coloured rug from chest to feet.

'This is my friend, Paolo Goldoni,' said Scott, leading her forward and introducing her. 'Paolo, Miss Lacey Kent whom I have invited to stay at the villa for the night. She has had problems with her hotel. I'm going to find her a more suitable one in the morning.'

Paolo Goldoni held out a small, claw-like hand.

'Welcome, Miss Kent. I hope we can persuade you to stay for longer than one night. We are very pleased to have you.' He looked up at Scott but his face was strangely expressionless.

'Let me show you to your room,' said Scott. 'You might like a rest before dinner. Gino will bring up your luggage and a cold drink. Or would you like some tea? I know what you English are like for tea.'

'I've spent little time in England for the past ten years. I haven't got the tea habit,' she said with a laugh. 'A cold drink would be lovely.'

★ ★ ★

Half an hour later, freshly showered and wearing a soft wrap, she sat on the balcony of her bedroom and allowed her hair to dry in the warm air. She had carried the jug of fresh lemonade on its bed of ice on to the balcony and now drank glass after glass thirstily while she studied her surroundings.

There were no houses nearby, but immediately below and to the right of the villa, on the edge of the cliff, she could make out the ruined top of an old building. It looked interesting. She would ask Scott about it at dinner.

The barking of a dog below her balcony made her leave her chair and look over. A small fluffy black dog was jumping about excitedly as a slim, brown-haired girl tried to attach his lead. At last she succeeded and they set off down a narrow path towards the trees.

The niece, Lacey thought to herself. For a second she thought there was something oddly familiar about the girl, then dismissed the idea as silly.

She returned to her chair and her cold drink. But she couldn't settle and decided to rest on her bed for an hour. Setting her small travelling alarm clock, she stretched out on the bed and in a few seconds, was asleep.

★ ★ ★

Scott was waiting for her at the bottom of the stairs when she went down to dinner. She was wearing one of her new evening dresses in a fresh design of blue and white daisies on a midnight blue background and had swept her long fair hair up into soft curls, a style which complemented the dress. Scott's eyes shone appreciatively as he swept her a low bow and held out his arm.

'May I take you into dinner, your ladyship?'

Lacey smiled at him happily. He

really was great fun. She was glad she'd accepted his invitation to stay at the villa. Together they entered the dining room where flickering fat candles illuminated old paintings and statues.

There was a huge stone fireplace filled with greenery and the ceiling was low and blackened with smoke.

Her host was already seated at the head of the long, black table, propped up by cushions. His niece, waiting near the fire, looked up as they entered. Again, Lacey had the feeling that she had seen her before. Then it came to her in a flash. She was the girl in the mirror at the airport; the girl whose reflection had looked blankly back at her. There was no sense of recognition now, though.

The meal was plain but delicious. Lacey found she was very hungry and Scott smiled to see her tackle every course with enthusiasm.

Paolo's niece, who was called Angelica, did not speak and ate little. Lacey thought she seemed nervous and indeed, she excused herself and left the room before the end of the meal. Her uncle watched her go but made no comment. Gino entered with a lemon pudding, and Lacey, tasting its exquisite, sharp sweetness, immediately forgot the other girl.

After dinner, Scott made their excuses to Paolo and took Lacey on to the terrace. The evening, though late, was still warm and light. They began to stroll along the paths of the garden, which, though so near to the sea, was vibrant with myriad brightly coloured flowers in terracotta pots.

Through the pine trees, they glimpsed the sea, now a deep vibrant blue, and across the bay, indistinct in the evening light, the glowering shape of Vesuvius.

Then Lacey remembered the old building she had glimpsed from her balcony.

'It's just here.' Scott pointed through the trees where some uneven stone walls were just visible in the fading light. 'It's a Saracen watchtower.'

'Which was . . . ?' asked Lacey.

'What it says. A thousand years ago, the Saracens invaded Naples. Watch towers were built at intervals along the coast which were manned day and night to give warning of the invaders.'

'And they are still standing, after all this time?'

'Some are in better repair than others. I haven't investigated Paolo's tower.'

'Oh could we go and see it, please?' asked Lacey, feeling almost excited.

'Not now,' he said sharply. 'It's getting dark. We'd better go back.'

'Are you cold?' She asked him

'No. But we should go back. We haven't phoned the hotels.'

She gave him a worried look. 'Oh dear, I forgot about the hotel.'

'You could stay here,' he suggested, lightly.

'No. I mustn't. I must find a hotel in Sorrento.'

He raised his hands in submission. 'Very well, we'll find you a hotel, or rather, I'll find you a hotel. I have a feeling your Italian isn't up to it.'

'You're right, it isn't. I have French and German, but very little Italian. Thank you. If you would phone for me, I'd be grateful.'

'Would you mind if I went to my room now?' she asked, as they entered the villa. 'I suddenly feel very tired.'

'Just go on up, then,' he said. 'Don't come down to breakfast. You can have it on your balcony.'

*　*　*

She slept well but woke early. The sun was bright through the gauzy curtains of her room. She swung her legs over the side of the high bed, reached for her wrap and shrugging her arms in, went out on to the balcony. The paved floor was already hot enough to burn her bare feet.

There was still some lemonade left from the night before. She returned to her room, poured a glass and took it with her to the balcony, perching on the low wall and throwing back her head so that the early sun could caress her face.

This was the way to start the day, she thought, feeling the sun gently warm all her limbs and bring them to life.

On the terrace below, the excitable little dog was being shushed by Gino. He looked up and saw her.

'Good morning. Would signorina like her breakfast now?' he called up.

'Please, Gino.' She found she was quite hungry. Must be the air. She finished her lemonade, washed her face and hands and brushed her hair and was waiting with a smile for Gino when he appeared with a tray.

The breakfast of fruit, toast and coffee was light but satisfying. She savoured each mouthful, sitting at a small table on the balcony with a view of hills on one side and the sea on the other. What would it be like to live always in these idyllic surroundings, she mused.

Scott was on the terrace when she eventually went downstairs. He pulled out a chair for her and offered coffee, but she shook her head.

'I've had breakfast, thank you. Have you phoned the hotels?'

He was silent for a moment, then he gave her his wide smile.

'I have,' he said, slowly, 'but without much luck. I really do think it would be best if you stayed here.'

'No. I must be in Sorrento.'

'Sorrento is very crowded.'

'But there must be a room some-where. How many hotels did you try?'

'You'd really be so much more comfortable here, you know' he said, smoothly. 'And as an added bonus, I can drive you wherever you want to go.'

'No,' she said, quietly. 'Thank you, but I don't want to stay here. Please take me back to Sorrento now or kindly call me a taxi. I'll find my own hotel.' Suddenly she didn't want to be with Scott, she wanted to be on her own. She stood up. 'Now, please Scott.'

He stood too and the smile was gone from his face. Suddenly his size was not reassuring, it was menacing.

'You will stay here, Miss Lacey, at least for a few days.'

Remembering the locked gate at the end of the drive, Lacey willed herself not to panic. There must be other ways out of the estate.

Scott read her thoughts. 'Don't think of escaping,' he said, 'you will be watched. You can go in a few days, perhaps at the end of the week. You will come to no harm. In the meantime, enjoy this beautiful old house and grounds.'

She stared at him mutinously.

'You have a comfortable room and the food is excellent,' he coaxed. 'All much better than a hotel.'

What would her mother have done? One thing was certain, she would not have shown her captor that she was afraid. Picking up her bag, Lacey gave Scott a scornful look, turned on her heel and returned to her bedroom.

She flung herself on her bed, fuming. What a fool. What an unmitigated fool!

She'd known from the first that she mustn't trust anyone. She'd warned herself to keep a watch on her tongue. But because Scott Marner had a familiar American accent, she'd let down her guard.

There was a tap at the door.

'Go away!' she shouted. 'I don't want anything to do with you.'

The tap was repeated and a soft female voice called, 'Lacey, please let me in.' It was Angelica.

Lacey opened the door just a tiny chink. 'Scott wants you downstairs,' Angelica whispered.

Lacey began to close the door again but the other girl inserted the toe of her shoe to prevent it. 'You'd better come,' she said, urgently. Her expression was tense and frightened. 'He doesn't like to be kept waiting.'

4

Lacey followed Angelica down the wide wooden stairs. The girl opened the heavy door to the salon, motioned Lacey inside, and disappeared. Scott was standing in the centre of the room, a friendly smile on his face. There was no sign of the menace of their earlier meeting.

'Miss Kent, do come in.' He indicated an oversized but comfortable looking old armchair and gestured for her to sit down. 'May I get you a drink?'

Lacey ignored the chair and the drink. 'What do you want of me?' she asked. 'Have you found me a hotel?'

'Now I thought we'd settled that,' he said, smoothly. 'You'll stay here in comfort for a few days and if everything goes well, you'll leave at the end of the week.' Lacey said nothing but continued to glare at him. 'That being the case,' he went on, 'you won't be needing your passport for a few days. Perhaps you would hand it to me.'

She ignored the request and clutched her handbag tightly to her side.

'I'm asking nicely, but I can take it by force if necessary.'

'Why do you need my passport?'

'It's a matter of identification. You'll see what I mean very soon. Now how about that drink?'

Defeated, Lacey sank into the armchair. Paulo was in his usual place in the window. He smiled his screwed up, wizened smile.

'I should like you to stay with us, Miss Kent,' he said. 'We get so little company here.'

I'll bet you do, thought Lacey, if you abduct your visitors.

Scott handed her a glass of some deep red liquid. She put it on the little table beside her, but had no intention of drinking it. It looked like red wine, but it could be something more dangerous. She had to keep her wits about her. Scott held out his hand.

'The passport, please. I promise you it will be perfectly safe.'

She looked at him. He was quite capable of helping himself. She unfastened her bag, extracted the passport and handed it over.

'Thank you.' He gave her his wide smile. 'Ah, here she is.' He looked towards the door which was opening slowly.

Lacey gasped at the figure which entered. Was it Angelica? Gone was the curly, brown hair and in its place, a long, fair plait. The eyes which flicked nervously at her, were as green as her own. Surely they had been brown before? Her suitcase had obviously been rifled; the girl wore Lacey's blue trouser suit. She gasped. Angelica had been transformed into her double!

There could be only one reason for it. Angelica was being sent to reclaim the formula from Uncle Max's friend. They thought that Lacey's passport would convince him of her identity.

Scott handed the passport to the girl who put it in her shoulder bag.

'Now don't forget,' he said, 'Giovanni Estrelli has never met Miss Kent. If he has a photograph or a description of her, the passport will convince him. Look confident at all times.' The girl said nothing but her expression was anything but confident. Scott ignored this.

'Gino will take you to Sorrento and you will get the next ferry to Capri. Get a taxi to Estrelli's villa at Anacapro, collect the formula and come back as soon as possible. Telephone from Sorrento and Gino will come for you.' He patted her shoulder. 'Then you can leave us as soon as you like.'

Angelica went over to Paulo who took both her hands in his and kissed them. 'You will be well rewarded, my dear,' he said firmly. 'Do not let us down.'

Looking straight ahead to avoid Scott's intense gaze, Angelica left the room.

'Don't forget your wine,' Scott said to Lacey, as the door closed.

'I don't want your wine,' she said. 'So you are a crook. I was a fool, wasn't I? A trusting fool.'

He just smiled gently.

'Why have you let me know exactly what Angelica is to do?' she asked.

'What harm is there in your knowing? You can't escape or telephone anyone. You will be watched until she returns.'

Lacey sat in silence for a while, thinking. Suddenly she realised with horror, something they'd overlooked. The password!

They thought that Giovanni would just hand over the formula to the person he believed was Lacey. But he wouldn't. He'd demand the password. Angelica would telephone Scott and he would make Lacey give him the password. And if she refused? She daren't think of the consequences of that.

The deep notes of the lunch gong reverberated outside the door. Scott stood up. 'Lunch! Are you hungry, Miss Kent?'

She was about to say that she wasn't, and refuse to leave the salon, but common sense told her that she'd think better on a full stomach and that if she managed to escape, it might be a while before she got another meal.

In the dining room, she ate her minestrone soup in silence. Escape! That was essential, and before Angelica made contact. But how? Scott had said she would be watched. If she managed to leave the villa, how would she deal with the locked gates? They were probably electrified. Did the fence completely encircle the estate? How could she find out?

'You are lost in thought, Miss Lacey.' Paulo was studying her.

'I was thinking of my uncle, actually,' she lied. 'I'm sure he will be very upset that I have failed.'

'Your uncle should have accepted the generous offer we made him months ago,' said Paulo gently. 'Then he would not have involved such a young girl in his scheme. You could have been having a nice Italian holiday.'

Lacey said nothing. Her soup plate was removed and a plate of meat put in its place. She looked up at the woman who served her. She was large and plump with a smiling face.

'Mrs Gino,' said Scott. 'She will be watching you. Don't be deceived by the smile. She understands very little English. And she will do as we say.' There was menace again in his tone.

After lunch, Lacey was taken back to the salon.

'What would you like to do?' asked Scott. 'We have plenty of books and magazines. Would you like to sit on the terrace? Or would you prefer a walk? It's not too hot and the grounds are shady.'

Lacey thought rapidly. If she went for a walk, she could size up the possibility of escape. She could run faster than the plump Mrs Gino. She had to get away. No one knew she was at the villa. If they needed the password, what might they not do to get it? She could disappear and no one would know she'd been there.

'I think I would like to take a walk,' she told him, 'I need some fresh air.'

Scott stood up. 'Very well. We'll take Luca. He hasn't had a walk today.'

Lacey's heart sank. So her companion was not to be Mrs Gino but Scott, who was more than capable of dealing with an attempted escape.

They set off, Luca racing excitedly ahead, then rushing back to them to jump up and lick their hands.

'He loves walks,' said Scott. 'Angelica usually takes him.' He was chatting as naturally as if they were merely friends.

'Shouldn't he be on a lead?' asked Lacey. 'He could run away.'

'No chance. The fence is electrified. He couldn't get out.' He smiled as if to say, and neither could you.

The day was beautiful, sunny, but not bakingly hot. The air was full of the scent of pine trees, overlaid with the ever-present perfume of lemons. In other circumstances, it would have been a very pleasant walk. But Lacey felt dejected. How could she escape?

If she managed the impossible and got out of the villa and out of the grounds, there was the added problem that the villa was so isolated. How could she get to Sorrento or anywhere else where she might get help?

'I think I want to go back now,' she said.

Scott whistled to Luca and they turned and walked back to the villa. They returned to the salon and Lacey sat miserably in one of the large armchairs. Paulo looked at her sympathetically.

'Do you like music, Miss Kent?'

'Music?' She looked at him blankly.

'Piano music?'

'Er — yes. I'm very fond of it.'

'Well I think we might be able to entertain you for a while. It will take your mind off your troubles.'

He gestured to Scott who took his

place at a grand piano in the far corner.

To Lacey's amazement, Scott was a superb pianist. His repertoire was light classical music and he changed effortlessly from one piece to another. Despite herself, she found she was gradually relaxing and when he stopped playing, half an hour later, her problems had receded to the back of her mind. But as he stood up, they came flooding back. She stood too.

'I would like a shower and a rest in my room before dinner,' she told Scott.

'Of course. I'll get Mrs Gino.'

'I don't need a jailer. I can hardly get out of the house without you noticing.'

He ignored her remark and left the room. Within just a few minutes he was back with Mrs Gino.

'I hope she doesn't intend to accompany me to the bathroom.' Lacey said tone was decidedly icy.

'She'll wait outside the door.' He spoke to the woman in fluent Italian. She smiled at Lacey, and for one fleeting moment, the girl wondered whether she could get her on her side. But she dismissed the idea. The smile meant nothing; she just had that sort of face. They went upstairs, Lacey thinking furiously. She went into her bedroom, lay on the bed and closed her eyes. Through her lashes, she could see Mrs Gino hesitate before sitting on a chair near the window.

Lacey picked up a magazine and began to fan herself.

Mrs Gino watched her for a while then unlocked and opened the French window. Lacey smiled at her gratefully.

There was silence in the room, then Lacey let out a faint groan. Mrs Gino looked at her anxiously. Another groan and Lacey rolled on to her side and brought her knees up to her chest.

Mrs Gino left her seat and approached the bed.

Lacey rolled on to her other side. Mrs Gino glanced at the door as if unable to make up her mind whether to summon help.

Lacey slowly rolled into a sitting

position on the side of the bed and sat, doubled up, uttering little moans.

She got awkwardly to her feet. Mrs Gino took her arm. Slowly, Lacey made her way to the bathroom, walking as if in agony. She went into the bathroom and closed the door, leaving an agitated Mrs Gino outside.

She sat on the edge of the bath and waited. She could hear Mrs Gino's heavy breathing. She sat for ten minutes. Then she heard, 'Mees Lacey. Mees Lacey.' She ignored the call. For another ten minutes, she sat. Mrs Gino was clearly perturbed. Standing near the door so that she could be clearly heard, Lacey gave a low groan, then another.

'Santa Maria!' She heard Mrs Gino hurrying towards the stairs. Lacey opened the bathroom door silently and rushed to her bedroom.

The Italian woman could be heard shouting, 'Signor Marner. Signor Marner.'

Lacey closed the bedroom door and locked it with the heavy iron key. She grabbed her shoulder bag, pulled it over her head and put her arm through the strap so that her hands were free. Footsteps sounded outside, then a heavy pounding on the door.

She raced to the balcony and looked over. There was no one in sight. Below the balcony was a low roof. Steps in the corner led to an area full of washing lines at the side of the villa.

Lacey climbed on to the balcony wall and dropped on to the roof below. Angry cries came from the bedroom. It would take Scott a while to try and break down the door and then he would probably give up and go back downstairs and out of the house.

Lacey raced for the steps in the corner and hid herself between the billowing sheets while she considered what to do next. It was no good making for the gates and the fence was electrified. There was only one hope. The seaward side.

The fence came up to the ruined watchtower and continued on the other side. The watchtower itself was built on several storeys going down the cliff. Was it possible to get out that way? Could she make her way along the beach? It was her only hope.

In front of the drying area were thick shrubs. She plunged into them, listening for sounds of pursuit. Taking a wild risk, she launched herself across the drive to another clump of trees and bushes on the far side. The watchtower was in front of her about twenty yards away. The bushes went almost up to the wall providing a good screen.

Hundreds of years ago, when the watchtower was in use, there had been paths down to the different levels of the building. The electric fence crossed what was left of these paths.

Lacey looked at them in consternation. She couldn't give up now.

What would her mother have done? She would not have given in, that was certain. She would have found a way to escape somehow.

Lacey studied the ruined Saracen

fort. Its roof was just six feet above the path. She could easily climb on to it. But would there be a way down from there? There was only one way to find out.

The corner of the building nearest to her was ruined and broken stones formed rough steps. She climbed on to it and cautiously raised herself enough to get on to the roof. The building was on the very edge of the cliff. What if it chose now to collapse into the sea below? As it had been standing for over a thousand years, she felt it was most unlikely.

Much of the stone roof was missing. She could see into the room below. It was too high to jump but there was the remains of a stone stairway. She decided to go down backwards, groping her way from stair to stair.

As she disappeared below the roof level, she saw Scott and Gino making their way along the drive from the house. She had no means of knowing whether they had seen her. For now, she must concentrate on these stairs and then try to get lower until she reached the beach.

There was only a faint light inside the building. The walls were thick and the windows tiny. She tried not to think what might be lurking in the dark corners.

Suddenly, as she reached the floor, she was grabbed from behind by a firm arm round her waist and a hand was clapped over her mouth.

5

'Don't scream,' warned an English voice. 'They're not far away and they'll hear you.' Terrified, she held herself rigid. The arm holding her gave her a shake 'If I release you, will you be quiet? Our lives could depend on it. Nod your head if you're prepared to do as I say. I only want to help you.'

Feeling that she had no choice, Lacey nodded her head. The man behind her removed his hand from her mouth. She turned her head. It was her 'stalker'.

His blue eyes glinted in the faint light from the small window. His hair was uncombed; there was stubble on his chin and his clothes were as scruffy as before. He didn't look like anybody's saviour.

'I want to help you,' he repeated.

'Why have you been following me?'

'It's a good thing I have. You couldn't

do much on your own,' he told her.

'Well what can you do?' Her chin came up defiantly. 'The gates are locked and the fence is electrified. How can we possibly escape from here? Tell me that if you are so clever.'

'How do you think I got in?'

She looked at him and changed her line of questioning.

'How do I know you're not one of the gang?'

'You realise we're wasting time. They'll put two and two together and come down here,' he said, irritated.

She didn't move and he sighed. 'Very well. The password is Maria Elena.'

'Who told you that?'

'Who do you think? Your uncle Max. Now will you come on?' He grabbed her arm and pulled her towards a small opening in the outside wall. Still holding her, he gave a quick look upwards. 'All clear. Come on. Down here.'

The path ran steeply downwards, past the building and towards the sea. There were doors and slit windows in the walls. The man stopped at the bottom door. He grabbed her arm again. 'In here.'

She stopped and held back.

'For goodness sake,' he said, 'we haven't got all day. I want you to see something — or rather, someone.'

As her eyes became accustomed to the gloomy light, she saw in a corner, a huddled shape in blue clothes. She looked at him in horror.

'What have you done?'

'She's all right. But I had to tie her up. We can't have her escaping and getting back to the house. She'll tell them what has happened, they'll know she's failed and come after you in earnest. At the moment, they think she's on her way to Capri and you are just trying to get away from the villa.'

'But how did you . . . ?'

'Questions, questions. I'll tell you everything later. We must get going. I'll phone the villa and tell them where to find her when we've got the formula and are on our way home.'

He checked the gag on Angelica's mouth.

'Don't want her screaming.'

Angelica looked at Lacey in mute appeal but she looked away. She was sorry for the girl but she was one of the gang. She followed the man out of the fort.

'Wait!' Lacey darted back into the fort. Angelica looked at her beseechingly but she ignored the look and bent to pick up the girl's handbag. She opened it, extracted her passport, dropped the bag and raced outside.

'Good thinking,' said the man, approvingly. 'You won't be able to get out of the country without it.'

They had come out on to craggy white rocks edging the vivid blue sea.

'Oh! I thought there was a beach,' she said. 'I was hoping I could have escaped along it.'

He gave a short laugh. 'No beaches here, just rocks and cliffs. There is only one way out and this is it.'

He led the way over the rocks and

down to the water's edge. Three small boats bobbed at anchor.

He jumped into one and untied the rope which secured it to an old iron ring in the rock. Holding out a hand, he helped her to scramble in beside him. He pointed to the stern and she clambered over a coiled rope and sat on the padded seat. He turned the key. The engine spluttered and died. He cursed and tried again. This time the engine growled then burst into life. He shifted the gears, bent low over the wheel, shouted, 'Hold tight,' over his shoulder and they were off.

I don't believe this, she told herself. I'm hurtling round the Bay of Naples with a strange man whom I thought was stalking me, but who says he wants to help me. I've been chased by a man who seemed friendly but is a member of a gang who probably want to kill me. For all I know, he may still be in pursuit. She looked behind. There were many small boats, but it was impossible to tell if one was following them. Uncle

Max could never have imagined this.

They were going fast, but she wasn't afraid. She was used to boats.

She looked around. The white rocks and cliffs gleamed in the bright sunshine. They passed umbrella pines and wizened olive trees, small caves and short, scrubby vegetation.

Here and there, a building, small and simple, clung to the most impossible pinnacle of rock. In contrast, large, white hotels, their windows winking in the sunshine, sat grandly gazing out to sea.

She turned her head and looked at the bay. The blue water changed to emerald then turquoise. The depths shone vivid green.

Boats rushed importantly to and fro; tiny motor cruisers and fishing boats, small steamers, and ferry boats. Large cruise ships lay at anchor. The man kept close to the coast, but not too close. Rocks beneath the waves were sharp and dangerous in the shallows.

This is ridiculous, I can't keep thinking of him as 'the man', she thought.

'What's your name?' she called. The wind took her voice away so she tried again, but louder. This time he heard.

'Rob. Rob Waring,' he answered.

They were slowing down now and he guided the boat into a tiny harbour and then cut the engines.

★ ★ ★

A few minutes later, they were walking with their arms round one another, through the harbour.

'We must look like a courting couple,' said Rob. 'The gang will expect you to be on your own.'

'You don't think Scott could be here?'

'Unlikely. But he's not a novice. He fooled you. Let's get you a disguise.' He darted into a tiny shop and came out with a straw hat with an enormous flopped brim. 'Pull it well down. It will hide your face.'

'Where are we going?'

'I have a friend here with a small bar. The boat is his. He has the most valuable and desirable thing in Positano — parking space. My hired car is there. We'll stay there for two days, then get a ferry from Sorrento to Capri.'

'Why don't we go to Capri now?'

'Once they find you've gone, that's what they'll expect you to do. If we wait, they'll think they've missed you.'

They walked on in silence, past the church with its colourful tiled roof and the fishing boats drawn up in rows.

'So this is Positano,' said Lacey. 'Isn't it beautiful. I've seen so many pictures of it, but it's even more spectacular than the photographs.'

Above them, houses painted white, cream, red, yellow and pink, rose up in tiers, clinging to the mountainside. Here and there, a car could be seen between the houses, making a slow journey to the road above. But the main way to travel around the little town seemed to be to climb the hundreds of flights of steps. Lacey hoped the bar wasn't at the top of the town.

Rob took her round behind the

church, through several alleyways and up three flights of old, worn, stone steps. He stopped in front of a small dark bar and went in, pulling her behind him. She sank into a chair grateful for the shady coolness of the room, while Rob went to the bar. He shook hands with a stocky, dark-haired Italian. Their conversation seemed to consist of bursts of laughter and much shoulder slapping.

The man came out from behind the bar and Rob led him over to Lacey. There were introductions and Lacey was promised a long, cold drink.

She and Rob sat opposite each other with their drinks and Rob sighed.

'We made it. We'll be safe here for a day or two.'

Lacey sipped her fresh orange drink. It was refreshingly cool. They were alone in the bar. She replaced the glass on the table.

'Why did Uncle Max engage a body-guard for me — especially without telling me? He said I would be perfectly safe.'

'He wanted you to have the satisfaction of carrying out your mission successfully, but he would never have forgiven himself if anything had happened to you. He was playing safe.'

'I suppose I have to be grateful that he was. I didn't do very well on my own, did I?' Lacey said sadly. 'I feel such a fool, trusting Scott Marner just because he had a familiar accent.'

'It was understandable,' said Rob.

She studied his face. The bright blue eyes which had glinted like pieces of ice in the old watchtower, now had the sparkling azure of the sky.

With a shave and a haircut, he could be quite attractive, she thought. He was looking at her with a faint, mocking smile on his lips as if he could read her thoughts. She coloured and picked up her glass again.

'Antonio has a room upstairs for you to use,' he said. 'It won't be very grand, but it will be clean. Shall I ask him to show you?'

'I would like a wash, thank you,' she

admitted. 'I feel filthy after crawling through that fort. I wish I had some clean clothes.'

'Wait, I'll talk to Antonio,' said Rob and went behind the bar to speak quietly with his friend.

'There's a small market near the harbour in the morning,' he said. 'We'll go out then and get you whatever you need.'

The Italian smiled openly at Lacey. 'I show you room,' he told her. 'Please come with me.'

Lacey followed him up some dark stairs to an unlit landing. He threw open a door and stood aside for Lacey to enter. It was a tiny room with a bed, a chair and a small table. On the bed were towels and soap.

'Is a comfortable bed,' said Antonio. 'When you ready, come down. My mamma fix a nice meal.'

She thanked him shyly and with a wide smile, he closed the door and she heard him go back downstairs.

On the table was a china bowl and

beneath it, a bucket and a tall enamel jug of hot water. She smiled to herself as she washed. It was like going back in time.

Refreshed, she combed her hair and applied a light make-up. She could do nothing about her grubby, white T-shirt, but she rubbed the dust from her shoes with a paper tissue.

'That's the best I can do,' she told herself. She left the room and began to make her way downstairs.

Rob was still sitting at the table in the bar where she had left him. Opposite him, sat a tall, well-built man with his back towards Lacey. His hands were on the table behind a leather holdall.

'Miss Lacey. Do come and join us,' said the man — it was Scott Marner. 'And don't try any tricks.'

Slowly she crossed to the table and slid on to a chair.

She looked at Scott's hands behind the bag. They held a gun, and it was pointing straight at Rob.

6

'I sure have to hand it to you guys,' said Scott, 'I would have thought it was impossible to escape from that villa.' Lacey sat biting her lip to prevent the tears which threatened to fill her eyes. To be so close to getting away.

'How did you know where we were?' Rob's disappointment and annoyance showed in his grating tone.

'Well now, I don't see why I should tell you, but I will. Gino and I saw you on the path past the fort. I guessed you were going down to a boat. Nowhere else you could go, really. So I followed you and Gino went back for the car. We kept in touch by mobile phone. When you came to Positano, I directed Gino here. He won't be long.'

'What are you going to do?' asked Lacey.

'We won't go back to the villa, that's

for sure. You didn't appreciate the luxury. And if you've escaped once, well ... No, I have somewhere far more remote. Nowhere near the sea and boats.'

Gino came into the bar. He flashed Rob a nasty look.

Scott spoke to him in Italian. Gino went to the bar and quickly tossed back a glass of lager. Antonio tried to chat but was ignored. Gino returned to Scott. Scott called something to Antonio in rapid Italian.

'I've told him that we're all going out for a meal. Gino has the car outside. You,' he nodded at Rob, 'will follow him. And don't try anything. You'll get in the front beside him. Miss Kent and I will follow and sit in the back. The gun will be on her all the time, so don't forget it.'

Lacey turned a scared face to Rob. He smiled and nodded as if to convey that she would be all right. With a gun so near, it didn't reassure her.

The little procession made its way

outside to where Gino had parked the car. Three vehicles, anxious to pass, were beeping their horns. Gino ignored them. The four were soon inside, and the car began the tortuous journey up the narrow street to the main road above.

There was silence inside the car. Lacey was afraid to move, conscious of the gun in Scott's hand. She knew that Rob would be planning another escape but she desperately hoped he wouldn't do anything impetuous in the car.

They turned off the road and began to climb up a side road through a small, deserted village of old sun-baked houses. The only sign of life was a large black cat on a wall which yawned as they passed.

At the end of the road, Gino swung on to a narrow track which led upwards through umbrella pines and short, scrubby vegetation.

'I take it you discovered the girl in the fort and released her,' said Rob at last.

'Of course,' said Scott. 'I'm sorry you went to such trouble for nothing. Angelica explained it to me briefly — what you did, I mean. Perhaps now you can tell me why.'

'Isn't that obvious?'

'You wanted to stop her from getting the formula. However I think there's more to it than that.'

Rob was silent.

'Anyway, it doesn't matter now,' said Scott. 'You failed. She's safely on her way there to collect the formula.'

Lacey drew in her breath so sharply that Scott looked at her. She turned her head away and looked through the window at the dried up vegetation. So she wasn't safe yet, she realised. Angelica would still contact Scott and tell him about the password. And why hadn't he mentioned the passport? She held her handbag tightly.

The car stopped abruptly outside an isolated house. There was none of the charm of Paulo's villa. The house had once been painted a soft peach but time and the weather had removed most of the paint. One of the windows was boarded up and a metal awning over the door was broken and hanging askew.

'I guess you wished you'd stayed at the villa.' Scott gave a mirthless laugh. 'Get out carefully, Miss Lacey, the gun is still pointing at you.' This was said mostly for Rob's benefit.

Gino opened the door and they went inside. The rush of air as the door was opened disturbed piles of dust. There was a musty smell as if the rooms had been closed up for some time. Gino opened shutters and light flooded in.

'In there.' Scott nodded towards a door in the far side of the dirty room. Rob opened the door and went in. Scott gestured to Lacey to follow. Gino came behind and opened the shutters in that room too. Lacey shuddered. There was a bed with a grim coverlet, a table and two chairs, and incongruously, a beautifully carved wooden sideboard. On the sideboard was a pile of books and old magazines. In the corner near the door was a cheap, single wardrobe.

'Not ensuite, I'm sorry,' said Scott. 'You'll have to call if you need the facilities, such as they are. I'm afraid you can't have separate rooms, the villa doesn't run to them. This is the only habitable room, apart from the living room and kitchen. 'But I'm sure you won't mind being together.' He opened the door and stepped through. 'You can plan another escape.' He gave a mocking smile before closing and locking the door.

* * *

Lacey and Rob stood in the middle of the room and looked at each other. Rob touched a warning finger to his lips. Scott could be outside the door.

Rob pulled out a chair for Lacey to sit down. He perched on the edge of the table near to her.

'I'm not proving a very successful

bodyguard, am I?' he said, ruefully.

She smiled bravely. 'You've done very well up to now. This is just a hiccup. You'll think of something.'

'What faith,' he mocked, but the smile he gave her was tender. He put a hand on hers where it lay on the table.

'At least you're not having hysterics,' he approved.

'Give me time. A night in this ghastly room and you don't know what I'll do.'

'We won't have a night here, I hope. Let me think.' He stretched his long legs out in front, crossed his ankles and stared at the floor.

Unsure what to do, Lacey wandered over to the window. The wooden frame was old, but iron bars assured that even if the glass could be broken, no one could get in or out.

Rob was watching her. 'There's no escape that way. We have to be a bit more subtle.' He beckoned to her to come back to her chair so that he could speak quietly.

'We need to know what sort of place

this is. What is at the back, and so on. If we ask to use the loo, we'll get a chance to go outside. It will be in the yard somewhere. You go first. Use your eyes. See if you can see anything useful.'

He banged loudly on the door and Scott soon appeared. Locking Rob into the room, he took Lacey through the dirty passageway, past the open door of the kitchen and into the yard behind the villa.

Lacey stumbled over broken paving stones and scrubby weeds to a foul-smelling lavatory in the far corner. Scott stood at the house door and waited for her. Facing the house were several broken down doors to outbuild-ings. One door was partly open and she could see a tarpaulin, but not what it was covering. The far end of the courtyard was open to the countryside which looked bare and inhospitable.

She made her way slowly back to the house, trying to look around as Rob had instructed.

'Come along, Miss Kent,' said Scott

impatiently. 'There's nothing to see here.' He began to usher her back along the passage when she stopped.

'I need to wash my hands.'

Sighing, he took her into the kitchen. Surprisingly, it was cleaner than the rest of the house. There was a cooker, a sink and a bare wooden table. She washed her hands, and refusing the towel he offered, dried them on a piece of paper towel. There was no sign of Gino.

'Ready now?' Scott's voice was sarcastic and she ignored him.

She was locked into the room and Rob was taken out.

'Gino will bring you some food later,' said Scott as he returned Rob to their prison and locked the door.

Rob was looking pleased with himself. 'Well?' His voice was quiet. 'Did you spot anything?'

'Nothing that would help us to escape. You obviously did.'

'I don't think it will help us but we know what we are up against.'

'What do you mean?'

'Did you see an open door outside?'

'With some tarpaulin? Yes.'

'A car,' he said. 'The tarpaulin was covering a car.'

'How could you see that?'

'I'm taller than you. I could probably see more. Enough anyway to work out that it was a car.'

'But how does it help us to know there's a car in an outbuilding? We can't get out of this room, and if we could, we couldn't move the car.'

'We know it's there, that's the important thing. Find out what you can about the opposition. It's vital when you make your plans.'

'And you have a plan?'

'Well no. Not yet. But I'll decide later whether that bit of knowledge will help us.' Lacey was sitting at the table and he joined her.

'We'll have to sit here all night if we can't escape,' said Lacey. 'Nothing would induce me to go near that filthy bed.' She shuddered. Then a thought struck her. 'How did you kidnap

Angelica and get her to the ruined fort? And how did you know where I was? You seem to have been very busy.'

'You could say that,' he grinned. 'I'd hired a car so I was able to follow you and Scott to the villa. I saw them lock the gate so I supposed you would be kept there. I drove to Positano and spent the night with Antonio and his mother. This morning, I left my car in the café parking space and borrowed Antonio's boat. Then I went back to the villa in the boat, made my way through the garden and on to the terrace. From outside a window on the terrace, I heard all the business about Angelica and the trip to Capri.'

The look she gave him was incredulous. 'You got through the garden and on to the terrace and even heard their plans from outside the window, and yet nobody saw you?'

'I've been trained to do that sort of thing.'

'Trained? Were you a spy?'

'No. Army. S.A.S.'

'Wow!' She looked at him with respect. Perhaps he could find a way for them to escape. 'What happened then?'

'I took the boat round the coast to Sorrento, tied it up and waited for Angelica and Gino. When they came, they talked for a few minutes, then Gino left her in the ferry queue and drove off. I persuaded her to come with me.' He grinned again showing even white teeth.

'What do you mean — persuaded?'

'She's a very nervous girl. I don't know where they found her but she wasn't a good choice as a conspirator.'

'Did you threaten her with a gun?'

'No. A banana.'

'A what? You're joking.'

'I don't carry a gun. I had a banana in my jacket pocket. Pressed into someone's side, especially if that some-one is already quite a bit scared, it feels just like a gun.'

'So she went with you as easily as that?'

He nodded. 'As easily as that. We

returned back round the coast to the ruined fort. I think she was almost relieved to be kidnapped, once I'd convinced her that I meant her no harm. It got her out of the plot and it wasn't her fault. Then you turned up.'

'But how did you know I would try to escape?'

'Your Uncle Max told me about your mother. I knew you would try.'

Lacey sat back in her chair. 'It sounds so easy, but I'm sure it wasn't.'

He smiled at her gently, then his head shot round and he looked at the window. 'Hush! The car!'

It was still and quiet outside. They were at the back of the house, but could quite clearly hear the sound of an engine starting up at the front.

'One of them is leaving,' he said. 'But which one? And why?'

The sound of the engine receded as the car moved away. They waited, looking at each other with puzzled expressions.

'Perhaps Scott is returning to the

villa,' Lacey suggested.

Rob didn't answer but sat, listening hard. A few minutes later, the sound of the car engine could be heard, getting louder.

'He's coming back. Where can he possibly have been in just a few minutes? There's nothing for miles.'

Rob slapped a hand on his knee. 'Of course. He's been up the track to turn the car ready for a getaway. This track doesn't lead anywhere. They have to turn the car and go back the way they came. They must have a wider turning place further up the hill. I wonder what they're planning now.'

'But going back to the subject of Angelica, you realise she doesn't know the password,' said Lacey.

'Of course, so Giovanni won't hand over the formula. Angelica will phone Scott, and if you'd still been at the villa, you'd be in trouble.'

'So you thought it best for her to disappear for a few hours,' said Lacey. 'Hence the kidnapping.'

'Exactly. But if they send her off again, there could still be trouble.'

They sat in silence for a while then Lacey looked at her watch. 'It isn't even beginning to get dark yet. At least we can see what we're doing.'

Rob checked his own watch. 'I imagine they'll bring us the promised meal soon. Do you fancy anything prepared in this filthy place?'

'The kitchen is quite clean,' said Lacey. 'After all, they have to eat here, so I suppose it would be.'

'He said that Gino would bring some food, didn't he?' said Rob. 'I have a plan. It's as old as the hills but it might work. Take off your top.'

Lacey wrapped her arms around herself. 'No!'

'Do as I say. It's our only chance. You'll be quite safe. Hurry up, he may be here soon.'

Reluctantly, Lacey removed her top.

'Your hair. Unfasten it and shake it round your shoulders. Now sit at the table with your back to the door.'

There were footsteps in the passage. 'Just in time,' hissed Rob. 'Put your elbows on the table and your head in your hands. Don't look at me.' He disappeared into the narrow space between the sideboard and the wardrobe.

The door opened and Gino came in with a tray. His glance fell on the forlorn figure at the table. The warnings he'd probably been given by Scott were forgotten. Without looking round the room, he approached the table and placed the tray in front of Lacey. She didn't move. He put out a tentative hand towards her, then stroked her hair, moving it aside to touch her shoulders. His hand moved lower. Lacey shuddered and in that moment, Gino dropped like a stone at her side.

Rob had leapt from his hiding place and with one sideways chopping movement, had knocked Gino to the floor.

Lacey grabbed her t-shirt and put it on.

Rob knelt and examined his victim.

He reached into the other man's pocket and extracted some car keys which he put into his own pocket.

'Only stunned,' he said, 'but he'll be out cold for long enough for our purpose. Wait here and be ready to dash when I say.'

'Where are you going?'

'To return the tray to the kitchen. Scott will be suspicious if Gino doesn't go back.'

'But if Scott is in the kitchen . . . ?'

'I'm sure he isn't.' He opened the door slightly and peeped out. 'I can hear music and it isn't coming from the kitchen. Now be quiet, we're wasting time.'

He picked up the tray and left the room. He rattled the key in the lock but left the door ajar. Lacey heard him call out to Scott in Gino's scratchy Italian accent, 'It's all right, boss.'

She couldn't hear Scott's reply but Rob came back without the tray. She gave him an admiring look.

'That was just like Gino. You should

have been an actor.'

'I was once,' he said. 'Not for long. I'll tell you about it sometime. Now come along — and don't make a sound.'

'What about Gino?' Lacey looked down at the man.

'Let him sleep. Scott will find him soon enough. For goodness sake, come on. We're losing our advantage.'

They crept along the passageway to the front door. Lacey held her breath as Rob turned the key. The door opened silently.

They were outside the house. Gino's car was waiting for them. Rob reached in his pocket for the keys and motioned Lacey to climb in the passenger side.

'Keep your fingers crossed,' he whispered. 'If it doesn't start first time, we're lost.' He turned the key, the car leapt into life. In two seconds, they were hurtling down the mountain path.

★   ★   ★

They shot through the umbrella pines, into and out of the still deserted village, and raced towards the main road.

'Is anyone following us?' yelled Rob.

Lacey turned round, craning her neck to see out of the back window. 'No.'

'We should have a good start,' he said. 'Scott will have to get the car out of its tarpaulin wrap, out of the courtyard and on to the road. And he'll have to move Gino; he can't leave him there.'

Lacey began to relax, despite their speed. If Scott had to do all that, they'd be bound to get away.

She took another look over her shoulder. At the top of the mountain path behind them, a large car was beginning the descent to the main road.

'Rob,' she almost screamed, 'he's coming. It's Scott.'

Rob swore under his breath, gripped the wheel more fiercely and pressed harder on the accelerator.

They had reached the main coast

road. Traffic streamed by. Rob had to stop and wait impatiently to turn into the incessant stream of cars and scooters.

'He'll catch us,' agonised Lacey.

'I can't help it. We don't want an accident. Right. A gap. Here we go.' He swung the car to the right.

Lacey looked behind them again. 'I can't see him, but there are too many cars for me to be certain.' She looked across at Rob. His lips were set in a determined line. He drove superbly, taking no chances, all his concentration on the job in hand.

Lacey smiled to herself. A few days ago, he was her 'stalker'. Now she had complete faith in him.

They began the descent to Sorrento. The traffic had thinned out. But the road was narrow and twisting and Rob daren't allow his mind to think of anything but the road ahead.

Lacey looked behind again. 'Oh no!'

Rob risked a quick glance across at her.

'He's behind us,' she whispered.

'Hold on.' They flew down the narrow road pursued by the other car. Lacey gasped as they took a particularly sharp bend. Behind them the screech of brakes was followed by a loud bang.

Rob stood on the brakes but it seemed an age before the car came to a stop.

'Stay here.' He jumped out and raced back up the hill. Cars coming up the hill towards Lacey used their horns to show that her car was in their way. In a moment, Rob was back and starting up the engine.

'Well?' Lacey looked at him anxiously.

'He went into the wall. The airbag saved him. I don't think he's badly hurt. People raced out of the restaurant opposite, so he'll get plenty of help.'

'What about Gino?'

'Didn't see him. Perhaps he was in the back.'

It was beginning to get dark. Now that they were no longer being pursued,

Rob could afford to take the twisty road and bends more slowly. They were soon driving through Sorrento and pulling up outside the San Gennaro Hotel.

Lacey looked at Rob. 'I don't have a room.'

He grinned. 'Leave it to me. The night clerk is a friend of mine.'

'Another friend?'

In ten minutes he was back. 'You can have my room. He's found me a room on the top floor. I've told him that if anyone makes enquiries, we're not here.'

He drove the car into the underground garage and parked in a dark corner. 'I don't think either Scott or Gino are in a fit state to come looking for the car, but we don't know how many accomplices they have. Come on, the lift's over here.'

Safely in Rob's room, Lacey sank wearily on to the bed.

'What a day. I feel exhausted.'

'Of course you do. Never mind, you'll soon be in bed.' He sat beside her and reached for the telephone. 'We must phone Giovanni and explain about Angelica and the password.'

He spoke into the telephone in his perfect Italian. He paused, and there was a burst of Italian from the other end in what Lacey could tell was a female voice. Rob spoke again then replaced the handset.

'Giovanni has been away for two days. He'll be back in the morning early. That was his housekeeper. She said that a young lady did call but she told her that Giovanni was away. She said she'd find somewhere to stay and call again in the morning.'

Lacey gave a heavy sigh. 'So there's nothing more we can do tonight?'

He smiled. 'Only sleep. I've asked Christo, my friend on the desk, to give us early calls.' He put his arm round her shoulders and hugged her to him. 'Your mother would be proud of you. All these hardships and no complaints from you.'

She smiled up at him, acknowledging

the compliment. He gave her a light kiss on the forehead and stood up.

'See you in the morning. A quick breakfast and we'll be on the first ferry.'

When he'd gone, Lacey gazed at herself in the mirrored front of the wardrobe. Her clothes had a decidedly grubby look about them. But what could she do? All her beautiful new clothes were at the villa. What would Uncle Max's friend think?

She showered and washed her hair, then washed her underwear. By now she was too tired to do anything but fall into bed.

Her last thought before falling asleep was that Rob had kissed her. How strange — and how nice. She touched the spot on her forehead with her fingertips and smiled to herself in the darkness.

7

Though it was early, the ferry to Capri was crowded. It docked at the Marina Grande and people surged ashore. Lacey wasn't sure what she expected to see — the name Capri sounded so glamour-ous and romantic — but it certainly wasn't this bustling harbour full of busy cafés, cheap stalls and itinerant sellers. And everywhere, crowds of tourists.

'Don't forget, it is August,' said Rob. 'If you want to see Capri in all its beauty you need to come well out of season.'

'Look! On that stall. T-shirts. I must get one and change. I won't be a moment.' Before Rob could say any-thing, she dashed away.

Clutching her new t-shirt, she hur-ried into a bar and was directed to the ladies' room. She returned to Rob wearing clean clothes and a wide smile.

'Should we phone Giovanni now?' she asked.

'Yes. We'll use the phone in the bar over there.'

Lacey waited anxiously as he dialled the number. It was answered almost at once. Rob quickly explained who they were and asked whether the young lady had arrived.

'Not yet,' Rob whispered to Lacey.

'When she comes, keep her in your house until we get to you and explain. We'll be as quick as we can.'

'Is anything wrong?' asked Giovanni.

'We'll tell you when we arrive. But don't let her go.' Rob rang off and hustled Lacey outside.

'There's a bus or a funicular railway up to Anacapri,' said Rob, 'but I think we'll take a taxi. That will take us straight to Giovanni's house and save time.'

'Where is Anacapri?'

'It's the other town on the island, above Capri town. Giovanni lives there.'

He hailed a passing taxi and they

climbed in. Lacey looked at it in amusement. It was surprisingly large for an island vehicle and could hold seven people. The top was open and covered by a coloured awning.

Rob spoke to the driver and they set off up the narrow, winding road to the town above.

'Just look at the view,' Lacey enthused as she gazed down at the azure Mediterranean a thousand feet below.

'Anacapri is more rustic than Capri town below.' Rob pointed to the olive trees and vines surrounding them. 'But it has some lovely houses and very luxurious hotels.'

'What a heavenly smell of flowers.' Lacey sniffed appreciatively. 'I wonder what they are.'

'Orange blossom and jasmine and, of course, the ever present lemons.'

'Anacapri isn't at the top of the mountain, is it?' asked Lacey, craning her neck to look upwards at the jagged white rocks towering above them.

'Monte Solaro. No it's halfway up.

But you can get a chairlift to the top of the mountain. The views from there are supposed to be incredible.'

Lacey sighed. 'If only we had time to look around. I can't believe I'm on the most romantic island in the world and I can't stay to see anything.'

Rob squeezed her hand. 'Perhaps one day we'll come back and see it at our leisure. After all, if you're on your own, you'll need a bodyguard.'

Lacey blushed and looked down again at the sparkling sea. Was Rob flirting with her? If he was, she found she didn't mind.

The taxi turned off the road, drove a short way along another narrower road and stopped outside a large, white villa. Rob asked the driver to wait for them and helped Lacey out.

They knocked on the studded, wooden door. It was opened immediately by a small, elderly woman, obviously the house-keeper. Without waiting for an explanation, she indicated a room opposite the front door.

A man was standing in the doorway. He came forward, smiling a welcome, with hand outstretched.

'My dear Miss Kent.' His accent was strong but his English was very good.

'Signor Estrelli. This is my friend, Rob Waring. Uncle Max asked him to accompany me for my protection.'

Rob shook hands. 'Signor Estrelli. First we must give you the password.'

'You and Max were both in love with Maria Elena,' said Lacey.

The older man nodded. 'Please come and sit down.' He led the way into the beautifully furnished salon.

'We spoke of a young lady on the telephone,' said Rob. 'I take it that she has not arrived yet?'

The other man smiled. 'But yes. I have her, as you say, under lock and key. Now you can tell me who she is.' He looked at Lacey. 'She is obviously supposed to be you.'

The housekeeper entered with a tray of wine and little biscuits. When they were settled, they told Giovanni Estrelli of their adventures since leaving London.

Giovanni's eyes twinkled. 'Oh to be young and have adventures. Me, I have a very boring life. But when I was young . . .'

'You and Uncle Max had adventures,' said Lacey. 'Maria Elena, for one.'

He laughed good-naturedly. 'Max was quite a one for the ladies. How is he now? Well, I hope.'

They talked of Uncle Max, then Rob recalled them to the present.

'Could I ask where you have the young lady?'

'She is in a very comfortable bedroom. She does not appear to be distressed at her imprisonment.'

'She is a reluctant criminal indeed,' said Rob. 'She is probably quite happy to be a safe prisoner.'

'Should we question her?' asked Lacey. 'Find out what she knows.'

'I doubt whether she knows anything of value,' said Rob.

'I will send for her.' Signor Estrelli rang a little bell and when his housekeeper appeared, asked her to bring the young lady to them.

When Angelica appeared, Giovanni looked from her to Lacey. 'Amazing,' he said. 'You could be twins.' He indicated a chair and Angelica sat down sullenly.

'You will come to no harm,' said Signor Estrelli, 'but we should like you to answer some questions.'

'I know nothing,' said Angelica.

'You must know something,' said Rob. 'Surely you know who asked you to pretend to be Miss Kent?'

Angelica stared at him and Lacey thought she was going to refuse to answer their questions. Then the girl gave a deep sigh of resignation.

'My Uncle Paulo. He and his friend, Mr Marner, wanted someone to pretend to be someone else, for a joke.'

'A joke!' Lacey sounded incredulous. 'A nasty sort of joke. I was kidnapped, threatened with a gun, locked up in a filthy house — all for a joke!'

Angelica ignored her.

'But you came here asking for a

formula,' said Signor Estrelli.

'That too was part of the joke.'

'This is ridiculous,' said Rob. 'We're wasting time with her. I think we should call the police and hand her over.'

'No!' Angelica looked terrified. 'No police. Please!' They all stared at her. 'If you call the police they will find out about Uncle Paulo. I will be in such trouble because it will be my fault.' She began to cry.

Giovanni Estrelli moved to sit next to her and patted her hand soothingly.

'There, there, Signorina. We shall not call the police.'

'But . . . ' Rob burst out.

'We shall not call the police,' Giovanni repeated. 'Signorina Angelica will stay here, locked in the room upstairs, in the care of my housekeeper, for a week while you both go back to London. Then I shall release her. She will be returned to her uncle and we will tell him that she was kidnapped, and she cannot be blamed for anything.'

Angelica smiled her thanks through her tears.

Rob raised his hands and then brought them down again on his knees in a resigned manner.

'Very well. If that is your decision. Now we should think of going back.'

The housekeeper was called again. Angelica was escorted upstairs and the bedroom door locked. Giovanni Estrelli went to a safe in the corner of the room. He opened it and took out an envelope.

'Now. Where shall you put this for safety?'

Lacey looked stricken. 'I had a special hollowed-out guide book,' she said, 'the formula was to have fitted inside. But I had to leave it at Paulo's villa when I tried to escape.'

'Don't worry. I'll carry it.' Rob took a waterproof envelope from his bag and slid Giovanni's envelope inside. Then he turned his back, slipped off his shirt and fastened the package to his chest. When he was dressed again, the package could not be seen.

Lacey smiled at him gratefully. 'What would I do without you?'

He made no reply but the look in his eyes made her blush.

*   *   *

Giovanni invited them to stay for a meal, but they were anxious to be off. If Scott Marner had recovered from his crash into the wall, he might yet be on their trail. Rob wanted them to be on a plane to London as soon as possible.

'If you could wait another ten minutes, I might be able to find out what has happened to your Mr Marner,' Giovanni ventured.

They both looked questioningly at him.

'I have a friend in the Naples police,' he explained, 'quite high up. He could find out what you want to know.'

'And perhaps where Scott Marner is now,' said Rob.

'Please sit down. I shall be as quick as I can.' The Italian left the room.

Rob and Lacey sat looking at each other and out of the window at the flower-filled garden. They both had the same thought. What if Scott Marner was waiting for them at the harbour?

Giovanni was soon back. They both stood up.

'I was lucky; he was in his office. Scott Marner is still in the hospital at Sorrento. He will be there for three or four more days.'

'And Gino?' asked Rob. 'Did you find out anything about him?'

'He was not with Mr Marner in the car. He was picked up at the house in the mountain. He has returned to the villa of Paulo Goldoni. As far as they know, he is still there.'

'Will they do anything about Paulo Goldoni?' asked Lacey. 'I think he was the brain behind the scheme to get the formula.'

'He has been known to the police for some time. I think there will be further investigation into his activities.'

'Thank you.' Lacey gave the surprised

Italian a kiss. 'Now we can enjoy the ferry ride back to the mainland.'

Promising to return to Capri and visit Giovanni again one day, they hurried out to the waiting taxi and were soon on their way back down the twisting road to the harbour below.

A ferry was waiting and they hurried on board. They found a table under an awning on the deck. Rob ordered cool drinks and they sat back and smiled at each other.

'I'm going to enjoy this sea trip,' said Lacey, donning her sunglasses and gazing out over the side of the boat at the sparkling sea. 'I don't think I noticed anything on the way over.'

'That's why I decided on the ferry back, rather than the hydrofoil even though it's quicker,' said Rob. 'We don't have to worry about Scott any more, and you deserve a rest.'

'If I fall asleep, wake me up,' said Lacey. 'The warmth of the sun and the throb of the engines are making me feel very sleepy.'

'Don't fall asleep,' he said, 'you'll miss the dolphins.'

'Dolphins? Where?'

'They'll be around. You must look out for them.'

'The blue of the sea is almost unreal,' said Lacey. 'Have you ever seen the famous Blue Grotto?'

'I have.'

'And is it really blue?'

'Blue and mysterious and beautiful. It shimmers.'

'I wish we'd been able to see it. Oh look! A dolphin! And another!'

Rob smiled at her excitement. She turned and caught him smiling.

'Do I look funny?' she asked. 'I'm sure I do. I wish I had some fresh clothes, I feel such a mess.'

'It's good to see you happy,' he said. 'You've had a dreadful few days. And it was supposed to be a holiday.'

'Well only partly a holiday. Mostly, a mission. And thanks to you, it's a successful mission. Shall we meet again, when it's over?' she asked.

'That depends on you. Would you like us to meet again?'

Lacey studied his brown, bristly face and untidy hair. Did he always look like this or was it part of his disguise? She could hardly say, 'I'd love to see you again if you looked more presentable.'

His blue eyes twinkled at her. She was sure he could read her thoughts. She turned away, confused.

'I have a feeling that we'll meet again,' he said, softly, almost dreamily.

The ferry sailed on towards the mainland between large rocks and mini islands which looked as if they'd been dropped into the sea by a giant hand.

'Sometimes the boat drops anchor so that people can swim,' said Rob.

'What a lovely idea. It looks very deep but it must be so cool on a hot day.'

All too soon they were off the ferry and climbing aboard the crowded bus which would take them up the steep hill and into Sorrento.

'Let me stop and get a change of

clothes,' she begged, as they left the bus. 'I can change at the hotel. At least I'll be clean for the flight home.'

★ ★ ★

At the hotel, while Lacey showered and changed into the long blue cotton skirt and white smock she'd bought in the town, Rob telephoned the airport. Lacey came into the room in time to hear him book two places on a flight just after nine, from Naples airport.

He looked with approval at her new attire. 'Very nice. Just the thing for a holiday in the sun.'

'But I'm not having a holiday in the sun! It will probably be raining in London when we get there tonight.'

'I'll just phone the car hire people to get them to collect their car from the bar in Positano,' he said, 'then we'll be off.'

'What about Gino's car?' she asked, when he'd finished.

'We'll use it to get to the airport then

I'll phone Signor Estrelli and get him to tell his friends in the police where it is. They'll see that Gino gets it back.'

They decided that they might as well sit together on the plane. They were known by the gang to be travelling together, so if they were seen, it wouldn't really matter.

Lacey still felt tired, so for the first hour she closed her eyes and slept. She opened them to see a large blond man, two rows in front, getting to his feet. She nudged Rob's arm in alarm. The man turned and made his way past them to the back of the plane.

Lacey breathed a sigh of relief. The man was nothing like Scott. She turned to Rob. 'Oh dear, I thought . . . '

'I know. Don't be so jumpy. If anyone is here, it won't be Scott Marner. He's safely tucked up in Sorrento Hospital.' Lacey closed her eyes again.

This time she thought back over the events of the past few days. Was it only a few days? Meeting Scott Marner and being so wrong about him. And being wrong about Rob, too.

She peeped, through half open eyes, at her companion, to find he was looking at her. His expression was gentle, protective; strange from such an 'action man'.

He reached out and clasped her hand. 'Nearly there. Are you glad?'

'I suppose I am. I don't think I could be an adventurer like my mother. But I'm glad I've had a taste of her life. Now I know I'm satisfied with my own.'

He was thoughtful for a few minutes, then he said, 'Is there anyone special in your life?'

'You mean, anyone . . . ? No. No one. Not at the moment.' She looked up at him. 'What about you? Is there someone special in your life?'

'No. I travel light. But that doesn't mean I won't change my mind. So far, I haven't met anyone who could make me change. At least, I don't think so.' He bent towards her and the intensity of his blue eyes deepened.

The instruction to fasten their

seatbelts saved her racing emotions.

They moved apart and soon the aeroplane touched down and was speeding along the runway.

*   *   *

Once in the airport, they hurried along the interminable corridors towards the exit. Lacey had to will herself not to look nervously around and view everyone with suspicion.

Outside, Rob hailed a taxi. 'I'll come with you to see your uncle. Well I must.' He laughed. 'I can't remove my shirt here.'

The streets were crowded, but in no time the taxi was pulling up in front of Uncle Max's imposing Victorian house. Uncle Max himself opened the door in answer to their ring. He began to tremble with anticipation when he saw them.

'Lacey, my dear girl.' He swept her into a bear hug. 'Tell me quickly, have you got it? I've been on tenterhooks.'

'I haven't,' teased Lacey, smiling at his expression, 'but Rob has.'

Uncle Max began to shepherd them into the drawing room, but Lacey motioned Rob towards a little cloakroom. He joined them a few moments later and handed Uncle Max the package containing the formula.

Uncle Max extracted it carefully, with trembling fingers, and studied the writing and symbols, his lips moving as he read. For a few minutes he was completely lost to them. Rob and Lacey chose armchairs, sat down, and waited.

At last, the old man looked at them, a huge smile breaking out on his face.

'I can't believe it,' he said, tapping the formula. 'This was created in the fifteenth century and now I have the chance to bring it back to life.' He sat opposite them. 'I want to hear all about it. Did you have any problems getting it?' He stared in surprise as they both began to laugh.

'Wait!' He put up a hand. 'There is obviously a story here. Let me order coffee and sandwiches and you can tell me all about it.'

Lacey related most of their adventures, stopping now and then to appeal to Rob for a detail or a confirmation. Uncle Max turned a shining face to first one then the other.

'So much in such a short time,' he marvelled. 'Your mother would be proud of you.' He patted Lacey's hand.

'I couldn't have done it without Rob.'

'I knew I'd chosen well when I first engaged him.' Uncle Max's tone was almost complacent.

'I couldn't understand why he hadn't accompanied me openly,' said Lacey. 'But perhaps this was the best way. He certainly confused the enemy.'

'I thought you might have managed alone,' said her uncle, 'but I had to be sure you were safe.'

★   ★   ★

When everything had been said, Rob offered to see Lacey back to her flat, leaving Uncle Max to gloat over his formula.'

There was a certain diffidence between her and Rob as they travelled to her flat. The danger and excitement which had bound them together was gone. Now they were two comparative strangers again and chatted of everyday matters.

'When do you return to your school?'

'I don't think I will. It was only a temporary contract anyway. I've decided to write to them tomorrow and say I won't be coming back. They really want a permanent teacher so they won't mind.'

He looked at her questioningly. She laughed.

'I think I've got used to a life of excitement. I want to stay in London. I don't want to be buried in the country.'

'What shall you do here?'

'I'll apply to an agency. My computer skills aren't too bad and I have French and German. It shouldn't be too hard to get something to do.'

'I'm based in London so I'm sure

we'll meet again soon.'

'Oh I hope so.' The words were out of her mouth before she could stop them. She flushed. 'What will you be doing next?' she asked hurriedly, to cover her confusion.

'I have several assignments lined up,' he said, vaguely. 'I'll be out of the country more than in it for the next month.'

They had arrived at her flat. 'I'm going to leave here in the next few days,' she said as she prepared to alight from the taxi. 'It's only a borrowed flat. I'll go back to Uncle Max. His house has plenty of room.' There, I've told him where to find me if he's interested, she thought.

They both got out and Rob signalled for the driver to wait. He accompanied her to the front door. They smiled nervously at each other. Then he put his hands on her shoulders and kissed each cheek, in the Continental manner.

'Au revoir, Lacey. I won't say goodbye because I know we'll meet again soon.' He was in the taxi and away before she could make any reply.

She opened the door and went slowly inside. There was a mirror on the hallstand. She gazed at her reflection. Was she the same person who'd left the building a few days ago?

Certainly she was carefree then. Now, she was not sure. Despite his rough exterior, she was sure that she and Rob could be soul mates. Did he feel the same way? His farewell had not been final, but was he letting her down lightly, pretending he wanted to see her again while having no real intention of contacting her?

She went upstairs to the flat. There were some letters behind the door, but none for her. She put them on the table and went into the bedroom. Life was going to be very dull. She hadn't even the pleasure of her new clothes. They were at Paulo's villa and lost to her.

Never mind, she thought. Tomorrow I must get my hair done and see about a job interview. Life goes on!

She picked up the photograph of her mother from the bedside table. 'Were you watching me?' she said to herself. 'I hope you were and I hope you thought I did all right.'

8

Lacey contacted several employment agencies the next day and made appointments at three of them. The second proved to be just what she wanted. The proprietor was American and they hit it off immediately. Lacey agreed to start work the following Monday.

She called at Uncle Max's house after work to bring him up to date with all her new plans.

'So I won't be going back to the school after all,' she finished. 'I've found a new job in London.'

'In London! Wonderful! I shall see much more of you, I hope.'

'Well, actually, Uncle Max, I do have to give up my flat at the weekend and I was wondering . . . '

'If you could come and live here? You do mean that, don't you?'

'Well I don't want to impose on you.'

'Impose! My dear girl, I would like nothing better. This house is far too big for one old man and two servants. You can have the two rooms at the back above my laboratory. They both over-look the garden. One has a French window on to a tiny roof garden. Perhaps you remember it? It would make a lovely sitting-room for you.' He chuntered on happily while Lacey smiled at him.

They took their coffee to the drawing room, Uncle Max still making plans for Lacey's stay with him. Then he stopped suddenly.

'I nearly forgot. Something arrived for you this morning.'

'For me?'

'Yes. A suitcase.'

'A suitcase? My missing clothes! The ones I left at Paulo Goldoni's villa. But how did they get here?'

'Courtesy of Giovanni and the Naples police, I should imagine. I expect Giovanni will write to me about it eventually.'

Lacey inspected the suitcase. It did indeed contain her new clothes. She sat down again and picked up her coffee cup with a pleased expression on her face. The smile disappeared at Uncle Max's next words.

'Have you heard anything from Rob Waring yet?' He was spooning sugar into his cup and didn't notice her expression change.

'I don't expect to, I'm sure he's busy.'

'But you'd like to hear from him,' he went on, wryly. 'I could tell. And he looked at you as if . . . '

'Uncle Max. Please! There's nothing between me and Rob Waring. Yes, I liked him, but we have totally different kinds of lives. He's out of the country a great deal. That wouldn't make him much of a companion.'

Uncle Max looked at her thoughtfully but said nothing more on the subject.

'Have you started the perfume?' she asked, changing the subject.

'There's a lot of preparation required

first. And I have to buy certain ingredients. I am — what do you say? — psyching myself up to it. The project is too exciting to rush.'

'I've never seen your laboratory. Could I see it some time?'

'Of course. I can show you now if you like. Not that there's much to see.'

'No vats of bubbling perfume?' she teased.

'That's not how it's done.' He led the way across the hall and stopped at a locked door. He took a key from his waistcoat pocket. 'Some of the ingredients are very expensive. I always keep the door locked.'

Lacey wasn't sure what she expected to see. Perhaps high dusty counters and sizzling Bunsen burners as in old films like Jekyll and Hyde. What she saw was white paint and stainless steel; a clinically clean room with spotless surfaces and huge fridges. One wall was covered with shelves containing dozens of brown glass bottles in all shapes and sizes. On a counter sat some intricate looking scales and boxes of rubber gloves and pipettes.

'Not what I expected at all,' she said, turning slowly in the middle of the room. 'I thought I would be able to smell perfume.'

'I'm afraid I make very little nowadays,' said her uncle. 'Sometimes I don't come in here from one week to the next. After a lifetime in the industry, I don't have the energy or the enthusiasm I used to when I was young.'

'But you are excited about Lucrezia's perfume?'

'That's different.' His eyes shone. 'That will be an achievement.'

'How do you make the perfume?'

'It's mostly done by weight. People think you simply put in a drop of this and a drop of that like a witch's spell. But no, we weigh the ingredients on incredibly accurate scales like these. Some ingredients are so strong we need only the minutest amount.'

Lacey looked at the rows of bottles.

'How many of those will you use?'

He laughed. 'Some perfumes can take up to fifty, but not this one. Probably about eighteen. When I create a new fragrance from scratch I don't know what I shall use. But for this, I have a formula.'

'So it will be an exact replica of Lucrezia's perfume.'

'No. It can't be an exact replica. Some of the ingredients they used then can't be used now because they are prohibitively expensive. We have to compromise and adjust. But it will be as near as I can make it.'

'So what is the most expensive ingredient?' she asked him eagerly.

'Probably orris, a kind of iris — the extract costs about twenty-eight thousand pounds a kilo.' He laughed at the surprise on Lacey's face. 'And rose and jasmine also cost a great deal.'

'Will you need any of those?'

'A tiny amount of rose and jasmine. Then to make it a little more exotic, cinnamon, patchouli, sandalwood and clove. And other things which are of course the secret touches.'

'I can't wait to smell it. When will it be ready?'

'First I make the compound, which is the concentrate, the heart of the perfume. The ingredients are blended together like making a cake. I leave it for two weeks to settle then put it through a filter. Then it is ready to be diluted with ethanol and bottled. About four weeks altogether.'

He patted her shoulder. 'That's enough questions for now. I've given you a very basic idea of perfume making. The reality is much more complicated and magical.' He led her towards the door. 'When it is finished, you shall have a tiny bottle for yourself. You deserve it.'

'I'll hold you to that,' she said, with a laugh. 'Imagine, Claudia Capua and I, the only two women in the world to wear this perfume.'

'Until her husband manufactures it. Then anyone can have it.'

They returned to the drawing room. 'Are you free on Saturday evening, my dear?' he asked.

'Yes. I think so. Why?'

'I have tickets for the ballet. Swan Lake. You can come?' He looked at her hopefully. 'We'll have dinner first,' he went on as she nodded. 'You won't mind going out with an old uncle instead of a handsome young man?'

'You're fishing for compliments,' she scolded. 'Now I really must go. I'm a working girl remember. I'll see you on Saturday evening. I'll look forward to it.'

At the front door, she stopped. 'Uncle Max, you don't think they'll still try for the formula, do you?'

'Everything is strictly under lock and key,' he assured her. 'They have no chance. We're home and dry now. Just forget them and their nasty tricks.' He kissed her cheek. 'Goodnight, my dear girl. Drive carefully.'

*   *   *

Saturday night was the first of many outings with Uncle Max, always in the best seats and always preceded by a delicious dinner.

He was excellent company, well travelled in his youth, with an excellent repertoire of stories and anecdotes.

But sometimes, at the back of her mind, Lacey had a treacherous thought that an evening with Rob would be even better.

Her erstwhile companion seemed to have vanished completely. She had half expected a telephone call; hoped for a note; desperately waited for a visit. Perhaps he didn't want to see her again. She told herself she must try to forget him and concentrate on her job, her outings with Uncle Max and her new home.

The rooms were already pleasantly furnished, but her uncle insisted on taking her out to choose new soft furnishings and ornaments which would be more to her own personal taste.

The shop assistants think I have a

sugar daddy, she thought with amusement, as Uncle Max wrote a cheque for their latest purchase.

* * *

One morning, she received a letter from her father, giving rather startling news. He had become very friendly with a lady who lived not far away, and was contemplating marriage. 'She's a very good cook,' he'd added as a postscript.

The wicked old thing, Lacey chuckled to herself. He's found someone to take over all the chores he doesn't like himself.

'I have a very comfortable life,' she wrote back. 'I have two lovely rooms and take my meals with Uncle Max. His housekeeper, Mrs Wragg, does all my washing and ironing too, so you see, I'm quite spoilt.'

A comfortable, indulged life, she thought, but one thing is missing — or rather, one person is missing.

Then suddenly, he reappeared in her

life. The telephone rang one evening.

'It's for you.' Uncle Max handed her the receiver.

'Is that the other half of the perfume recovery team?' asked a voice.

'Rob! Oh Rob, it's lovely to hear from you. Where are you?'

Uncle Max smiled and tiptoed from the room, closing the door.

'Not far from you,' said Rob. 'At the airport. I've been out of the country since I saw you last.'

Lacey's heart was beating fast. She tried to speak casually. 'I wondered whether you were still around.'

'Would you be free tomorrow evening?'

I can't play hard to get, Lacey told herself. I must see him. 'I've nothing planned for tomorrow evening,' she replied.

'Good. I'll pick you up at seven. We'll have dinner and talk. But I warn you, I look a bit different. Oh and don't dress up, we won't be going anywhere grand.'

Disguise again, I suppose, thought Lacey resignedly. But please, not a shaven head.

★ ★ ★

Her plea was answered when she opened the door the following evening. Rob still had plenty of hair on his head — and on his chin. He sported a large bushy beard which almost covered the bottom half of his face. Her mouth dropped open, but she recovered quickly and took him in to see Uncle Max. Her uncle was made of sterner stuff and greeted Rob as if he noticed no difference.

In the car, speeding towards town, Rob began to laugh. 'Your face! Have you never seen a beard before?'

'I've never been out with someone with a beard like that before,' she retorted.

He stroked it thoughtfully. 'It took me two weeks to grow. It was necessary for my last assignment.'

'Can't you shave it off now?'

'I've become rather fond of it. And I'm not sure where my next destination will be. A beard might be useful.'

152

'Are all your assignments secret?'

'Not all. But I don't like to talk about them. Least said, soonest mended is always a good motto.'

So what are we going to talk about all the evening, Lacey thought as she got out of the car?

But by the end of the evening, she was surprised by how many topics they'd covered, from her new job to her new rooms; from her father's news to the making of perfume.

Rob talked little about his own activities. She dragged out of him that he had one sister who was a nurse in Manchester and that his parents had a hotel on a Scottish island.

'Does an Italian restaurant bring back good thoughts or bad?' asked Rob.

Lacey looked around. 'Well we didn't get to eat in a real Italian restaurant while we were there,' she answered. 'But the waiter's accent makes me feel as if I'm back in Italy again.'

The waiter placed large plates of spaghetti covered in fragrant tomato sauce in front of them. 'Italian food at its simplest,' said Rob, 'but delicious.'

Lacey agreed. 'But I wish I was more skilled at eating it. I'm almost tempted to use a knife and fork.' She watched as Rob twirled the spaghetti effortlessly round his fork. 'You're a real expert.'

'Eat it any way you like,' he said, 'but enjoy it.'

The table candles in the tiny bistro were burning low when he took her hands. His blue eyes sparkled in the flickering lights.

'Have you thought about me while I've been away?'

'Thought about you?' she repeated, stalling for time.

'Yes. I've thought about you constantly. The way you accepted all the problems we came up against without complaint. Not many girls would have reacted the way you did. You'd make a good partner for a man who liked an active life.'

You, for instance? she thought. Goodness, this isn't a proposal, is it?

'Say something,' he urged, as she remained silent.

She took a deep breath. 'I behaved as I did in Italy because I had the example of my mother in front of me. I didn't want to let her memory down. But I'm not an action girl. And . . . ' she swallowed, 'I don't want an action man as a partner, if you mean a partner for life. The glamour would wear off very quickly. I want a companion, someone who'd be with me to share my everyday life, to . . . to help me raise a family. Not someone who was goodness knows where in the world, possibly in danger or . . . ' She couldn't go on and was appalled to feel tears rolling down her cheeks.

'Lacey, please don't cry.' He took out a pristine handkerchief and gently dabbed at her cheeks.

'I'm not crying.' She grabbed his handkerchief and furiously rubbed her eyes. 'I'm mad with myself for imagining that you meant anything like . . . It was just a remark, wasn't it? Forget what I said. Let's change the subject.'

Rob sat back and beckoning to the waiter, ordered two coffees. Lacey breathed deeply to steady her voice.

Then she began to talk about a film she'd seen with Uncle Max, set in the part of Italy where they'd just been. Rob joined in as if the embarrassing scene had never occurred and soon Lacey felt calm again.

They left the restaurant soon after. They were both quiet as he drove her home. He refused to come in and said goodnight on the doorstep, bending to kiss her gently on the lips.

'Goodnight, Lacey. I'll be in touch when I get back.'

Uncle Max had retired for the night. Lacey locked the door and went slowly upstairs. In her bedroom, she sank on to the stool in front of the mirror. She put her elbows on the dressing table, her chin on her hands, and studied her reflection carefully.

What did he really mean? Was he talking of marriage? Was it a proposal?

She smoothed her eyes, still faintly red from the tears, with her fingertips, embarrassment flooded up at the memory.

If it had been a genuine proposal, what would she have answered? She couldn't marry a man who wore a bushy beard one moment, and a stubbly face the next. Who disappeared across the world on mysterious missions and wouldn't talk about them. A man who couldn't appreciate that she'd had an unstable childhood, forever moving from place to place. She wanted stability, however dull that seemed. She meant what she'd said. She wanted a companion — a normal, unadventurous man.

'Do you?' she asked herself out loud, 'Or do you want Rob?' These things had made Rob the man he was, the man she loved. She stared at herself in amazement. The man she loved! Her subconscious had decided.

She moved away from the mirror in a dream, prepared for bed and slipped under the duvet.

'The man I love,' she whispered to herself. Darling Rob, hurry back so that I can tell you.

But as her eyes began to close in sleep, a dreadful thought struck her. Was it too late? If Rob believed what she'd said, she might never see him again.

9

The outings with Uncle Max ceased for the moment as he became more and more occupied with Lucrezia's Secret, as she had learned the perfume was to be called. Most evenings he disappeared into his laboratory, leaving Lacey to sit alone, fretting about Rob.

She'd not had contact with him since their evening out at the bistro. He must be out of the country again. Or had he decided not to contact her?

One evening, when he'd been out all day, Uncle Max arrived home carrying a small parcel. He placed it, with great care, on the table in the drawing room, and looked solemnly at Lacey.

'When we have finished dinner, I shall show you what is in the parcel.' He went out of the room wearing a very satisfied expression.

After dinner, Lacey poured them

both a cup of coffee and waited. Her uncle produced a bottle of brandy.

'This is in the nature of a small celebration,' he said. 'We shall have a drink with our coffee.'

'Now,' he began to open the parcel, 'what do you think of this?'

He lifted from the velvet bed in the box, an exquisitely carved glass bottle. Within the glass was a fine gold mesh, suggestive of the clothes of a medieval lady. The stopper was of gold and in the very top, was embedded a large garnet.

Lacey drew in her breath, slowly. 'Uncle Max, it's quite beautiful.'

'It's a one-off,' said her uncle, 'specially commissioned. When the perfume is commercially produced, the bottles will be similar, although of course, not nearly so expensive.'

'Claudia Capua is a lucky woman,' said Lacey, stroking the bottle wistfully. 'Imagine having a fiancé so wealthy that he could commission this for you.'

Uncle Max returned the bottle to its

box. 'She demands the most expensive, and the best. Just like Lucrezia Borgia.'

After a while, he asked tentatively, 'May I ask whether you have heard from Rob Waring lately?'

Lacey sighed. 'Not since we went out for a meal. He did say that he was going away again. The trouble with him, you never know where he is. Not even which country he's in.'

'You miss him?'

Lacey sipped her brandy thoughtfully. 'When I first met him, I thought he was stalking me. And I didn't like his appearance. He looked scruffy and untidy. When I realised he was dressing the part, making himself look not worth bothering about, I understood why he looked like that.

'As time went on, I realised he had other qualities: he was brave and fearless, quick to work out strategies and capable in so many ways. If it hadn't been for him, I might actually have been seriously injured — or perhaps even killed.

'As we spent more time together, I realised that I liked him a lot. But I could never like his erratic lifestyle.' She sighed again. 'So I suppose the answer is, yes, I like him and I miss him. And he has lovely eyes,' she added with a smile.

'You need something to take your mind off him,' said her uncle. 'I've left you alone a lot lately. Shall we play backgammon for an hour or so? You beat me last time and I want my revenge.'

He sat back in his chair and watched Lacey set out the counters on the board between them.

'The perfume is nearly ready,' he said. 'A few more days and I shall decant it into the bottle. And then, a week later, you will have a surprise.'

My own bottle, Lacey thought. He's forgotten he promised it to me. Dear Uncle Max. She picked up her dice and rattled them in her hand.

'My throw, I think,' and she threw them across the board.

★ ★ ★

The perfume was ready. Uncle Max had done the final filtering and decanted it carefully into its crystal bottle. It lay in its velvet box awaiting the Italian actress for whom it had been created.

'Will it be collected or do you have to deliver it?' asked Lacey.

'Mr Denier, her fiancé said he will call for it on Thursday evening. I shall be glad when he has it safely in his possession. And the formula.'

On Thursday evening, Uncle Max found it difficult to settle. Lacey had continued to reassure him that the perfume was perfect, but he couldn't relax until Mr Denier approved it.

'Put on your green velvet dress,' he said to Lacey. 'I always thought you look very elegant in that.'

'Why must I look elegant, Uncle? He's coming to collect his perfume, not to look at me.' She laughed.

'But he is used to beautiful women.

You want to look your best.'

Lacey cast her eyes upwards but went to change. What a fuss, she thought. He's not coming to see me. He'll probably not notice me.

To please Uncle Max, she slipped into her green dress and coiled her fair hair on top of her head. She took care with her make-up and when she looked at the finished result in the mirror, she was pleased she'd made the effort. She went downstairs and joined her uncle in the drawing room. Almost at once, the bell at the front door rang loudly.

They listened and heard a man's deep voice speaking to the housekeeper. The drawing room door was held open and in swept the most beautiful woman Lacey had ever seen. The skirt of her long, coffee coloured dress swirled from a beautifully draped bodice. Her hair was drawn back severely into a chignon and her make-up was pale and perfect.

Lacey's first thought when she saw her was silently to thank Uncle Max for asking her to change into her best dress.

How could she possibly have sat in the room with this exquisitely gorgeous creature in only her everyday clothes?

'May I introduce my fiancée, Miss Claudia Capua,' said Charles Denier in his rich baritone voice.

Claudia smiled at them both then singled out Uncle Max. 'I am so excited about my perfume,' she said, in a heavily accented English. 'It has been so hard to wait for it.'

Introductions were performed and they all sat and looked at the box which Uncle Max had placed on a coffee table in the centre of the room.

'Before you open your perfume, Miss Capua, may I say one or two things,' said Uncle Max. 'Perfume is a very personal thing. It is one of the world's most sensuous creations. The nose singles out different sensations in a fragrance and one which can appear rich and exotic on one person, can seem flat and uninteresting when worn by another.'

'You wanted a re-creation of the

perfume worn by Lucrezia Borgia. As far as it is possible, I have done this. But I must warn you that you could dislike it, you could be disappointed. If I created a perfume for you, it would probably be nothing like that. This was created for a medieval lady.'

He picked up the box and handed it carefully to Claudia. 'Your perfume, signorina. Lucrezia's Secret.'

Claudia clasped her hands together in ecstasy, then she carefully lifted out the glittering bottle. They all watched intently as she removed the stopper, dabbed a little scent on her wrist, closed her eyes and inhaled.

Lacey was conscious of the ticking of the clock on the mantelpiece as they waited. Then the film star opened her eyes and gazed at Uncle Max.

'This is beautiful,' she said. 'So beautiful. Thank you.' She turned to Lacey. 'It will compliment my dress which is a medieval style. Try it yourself.' She handed over the bottle.

Lacey put a little on the inside of her

wrist. For this, she and Rob had endured several days of discomfort and danger. Was it worth it? She sniffed at her wrist, then smiled a slowly widening smile at her uncle.

'It's perfect,' she whispered.

The general air of tension lessened. 'Looks as if you've pleased two ladies already,' said Charles Denier. 'We must drink to celebrate.'

He took from a side table, a bottle which he had brought in with him. Uncle Max produced glasses and soon they were all drinking Charles's expensive champagne and laughing and chatting like old friends.

I shall wake up soon, thought Lacey. I shall wake and find I am not chatting to a film star and a millionaire as if I knew them well.

Uncle Max turned to Charles Denier. 'Would you permit,' he asked, 'that I give my niece a small bottle of this perfume? But for her, Lucrezia's Secret would not be here.'

'You must explain what you mean,'

said Charles. 'But of course you may give your niece a bottle.'

From a drawer, Uncle Max took a box and handed it to Lacey.

It was a tiny version of the other box and inside was a miniature of Claudia's scent bottle. Lacey speechlessly beamed her thanks to her proud uncle.

'Ah, but she must tell you herself,' said Uncle Max. 'She had the experiences. It is her story.'

Embarrassed at first, but gradually forgetting her shyness, Lacey launched into the story of her adventures in Italy. Claudia's eyes shone.

'But you are so brave. Me, I could not do anything like that.'

'It is like an adventure in a thriller,' said Charles. 'Miss Kent, we are eternally in your debt. And now, if you will both forgive us,' he stood up and held out a hand to Miss Capua, 'I'm afraid we must go. We are expected at a supper party in half an hour.'

When they had gone, Lacey and her uncle sat and looked at each other. 'It seems a bit flat now it's over,' said Lacey.

Her uncle was looking very pleased with himself. 'Mr Denier has been most generous,' he said, waving a cheque. 'I shall pay a large part of it into your bank. Without you, there would be no Lucrezia's Secret.'

'And without Rob,' she reminded him.

★   ★   ★

A week or so later, Lacey arrived home from work to find Uncle Max in a particularly good mood and humming to himself as he worked in the garden.

He had a fine herb garden; herbs such as thyme and lavender were used in making his perfumes.

'Smell this.' He brushed his hand over a sage bush. 'Close your eyes. Have you ever smelt anything so evocative of an English garden?'

Lacey was pleased to see him so cheerful. Since handing over Lucrezia's

Secret to Claudia Capua, he had seemed at a loose end, unable to settle to any other occupation.

'What is that?' She pointed to a tall plant.

'Ah, that's a surprise. Smell it.'

'Goodness, it smells of chocolate.'

'That's right. Cosmos, the chocolate plant. And what does this remind you of?' He broke off a few soft green leaves and rubbing them together, gave them to Lacey to smell.

'That's easy. Peppermint.'

'We'll make a nose of you yet,' he chuckled, leading the way into the house.

'A nose?' she queried.

'A nose is a person who can identify hundreds of different scents.'

After dinner, he asked her what she intended to do that evening.

'Someone at work told me of a good gym not far from here. I thought I might go and investigate.'

'No,' he said, abruptly.

Her head jerked up in surprise.

'I'm sorry, I just meant I hoped you'd stay in and watch something on television with me,' he added weakly.

'But you don't even like television, Uncle. You know that.' She laughed.

'This is different, and I want us to watch it together,' he said, mysteriously.

'Are you up to something, Uncle Max? This sounds rather peculiar.' She followed him into the small room where he kept the television.

'Sit there,' he instructed, indicating the armchair nearest the screen.

Of course, she thought, it's the perfume. Someone has the story. Well it doesn't matter, it isn't a secret now anyway. Claudia Capua will use it for publicity, I expect.

Her thoughts ran on as a programme came to an end and the next began. The title, Book Chat, came up on the screen and changed to the face of the presenter, Roy Pennell.

Lacey looked at Uncle Max, but he pointed sternly at the screen. He looked as if he was hugging himself in anticipation. Lacey smiled indulgently.

Roy Pennell made some comments about the Booker prize, promised details of a writing competition later in the programme, then picked up a book with a brightly coloured dust cover.

'Tonight, we have an interview with an exciting new young thriller writer. His first book will be on the bookshelves next week so I'd like you to meet — Robert Waring.' He held out a hand, and on to the set walked a smiling Rob.

'It can't be,' said Lacey. 'I don't believe it. It's Rob! Uncle Max, it's Rob!'

Uncle Max wore a smile wide enough to split his face in two.

'But how . . . when . . . ? How did you know? Why didn't he tell me? Oh dear, we're missing what he's saying.'

'Don't worry, I'm recording it for you.'

At last they settled to listen to the interview.

'The book is called, Songs of Araby,'

172

said the interviewer. Rob nodded.

'You did a lot of research in that part of the world? How did you get around? It must have been risky.'

'I was disguised,' said Rob. 'It can be dangerous for a westerner in some remote parts. I grew the beard which, as you can see, almost covers my face.'

'I'm sure our female viewers will have noticed your blue eyes,' said Roy Pennell teasingly. 'What did you do about them?'

'Dark brown contact lenses,' said Rob. 'It worked very well.'

'I understand you've had some very exciting news this week.'

'Yes. I can hardly believe it. Meteor Films are interested. They're trying to get some directors and screenwriters on board. Of course, it may come to nothing, but it's an exciting idea.'

'Have you started your next book?'

'I'm tossing ideas about in my mind,' he told her. 'It will be set in Italy this time. On the Isle of Capri.'

The interview ended a few minutes

later and Lacey threw herself backwards in her chair and covered her face with her hands.

'I can't believe it. Rob, a thriller writer. I thought he was a bodyguard.'

'He can be both,' said Uncle Max teasingly. 'The one job gives him plenty of ideas for the other.'

'Wait till I see him,' said Lacey. 'Keeping this from me.' Then she sat up slowly, an awful thought striking her. What if she didn't hear from him? What if her outburst the other night had put him off?

She stood up. 'I think I'll go to my room for a bit,' she said, embarrassed. 'I have some clothes to sort.'

'Lacey.' Her uncle called her back as she reached the door. 'Don't worry, he'll be in touch.'

* * *

The telephone rang as she was preparing for bed.

She had spent a tortured evening,

sure she would never see him again. He might not forgive her for what she had said. He might become famous and wouldn't want to know her. He might . . .

She ran into her little private sitting room as the telephone rang out and snatched up the receiver.

'Lacey? I'm sorry to ring so late. I just couldn't get away any earlier. Did you see the programme?'

'Yes, of course.' She suddenly felt shy. This was a new Rob. Her old partner in adventures was gone. This was a man on the verge of success, possibly fame. 'Uncle Max and I watched it together.'

'What did you think? Did I sound confident?' He gave an oddly boyish laugh. 'I was so nervous.'

Suddenly she wanted to tell him how she felt, how proud she was of him. But before she could begin, he broke in apologetically.

'Lacey, you sound tired. It's late. We'll talk tomorrow. Will you let me take you to dinner? We'll go somewhere really special to celebrate.'

'I'd like that.'

'I'll collect you at seven. Until then, goodnight, my love.'

She replaced the receiver and sat looking at the telephone. Goodnight, my love, he'd said. Please let him mean it.

'Goodnight, my darling Rob,' she whispered.

★　★　★

She woke with Rob's words in her ears. 'We'll go somewhere really special.' That didn't mean a small bistro. What could she wear?

She lay for a while reviewing her wardrobe. The green velvet? Too severe. The blue and white? Too summer holiday-ish. There was nothing for it, she'd have to go shopping in her lunch hour again.

Luckily the office was central. There were plenty of shops nearby. But she only had an hour, not long enough for window gazing. She marched resolutely down Bond Street heading for a department store at the far end.

A beggar curled on a pile of old blankets, held out a grimy hand. She was about to pass him, when the face of a grubby little white dog peered out from under the blankets. It looked so endearingly sweet she was unable to resist it.

Unable to ignore him, but tutting to herself at the delay, she felt for a coin in her pocket. As she handed it over, she looked up at the window above the man.

There it was! The dress she had hoped to find. At the back of her mind, she'd been thinking of the lovely gown worn by Claudia Capua.

The colour would suit her too.

In a dream, she entered the shop and spoke to the shop lady. Ten minutes later, she was gazing at her reflection in a huge mirror at the back of the shop. The dress was coffee coloured and scattered down one side of the floating skirt, were huge leaves in shades of bitter chocolate.

Uncle Max had been generous with her share of Mr Denier's cheque. A large amount of money was sitting safely in her bank, waiting for an occasion such as this. She had to have the dress, whatever the cost. She left the shop swinging a black and gold carrier bag and wearing an excited smile.

She intended to give the beggar another coin, but he had gone. Well he's played his part, she thought gratefully.

* * *

She was ready well before seven. She floated down the stairs and into the drawing-room. Uncle Max gazed at her for a full minute in silence.

'If that young man doesn't propose to you tonight, he doesn't know a beautiful girl when he sees one,' he said, with feeling.

'Uncle Max! He's not going to propose to me. What an idea.'

Yes, what an idea, she thought, what a wonderful idea.

There was a ring at the doorbell. Mrs Wragg showed Rob into the room. It was hard to know who was the most impressed; Rob, with the vision of loveliness who stood waiting for him in the middle of the room, or Lacey, who had never seen an immaculate Rob in a dinner jacket before. Gone was the bushy beard. His hair had been neatly trimmed, his shirt was gleaming white. They gazed at each other in wonder. Uncle Max broke the silence.

'Perhaps you'd better get going then you might think of something to say to each other.'

The two young people laughed. 'Would you like to come with us, sir?' asked Rob politely. 'It's a celebration. The perfume, my book, Lacey's new job . . . '

'And be a gooseberry? I think not. But thank you for the offer. Have a wonderful evening. I won't wait up for you,' he said to Lacey.

Rob had a taxi waiting outside. 'I think this will be a champagne evening,' he said, 'so I don't want to drive.'

Champagne evening, she thought, as they drove through the crowded streets. Yes, we have so much to celebrate: the successful end to our adventures, Claudia Capua's pleasure in her perfume and now his book, and maybe, a film. She smiled across at the new handsome Rob and he returned her smile as if he read her thoughts.

The taxi eventually pulled up outside a small, discreet and obviously expensive hotel in a square set just off one of the busiest roads in London.

'Roy Pennell recommended this place,' said Rob, 'and he should know. It has lots of awards and gold stars, so we should enjoy ourselves.'

He guided Lacey up the steps and through a gleaming black door with carriage lanterns on either side and a black and white awning above.

They were conducted through the hotel to a large, sunken conservatory at the back. Lacey's dress swirled about her as she descended wide stone steps and was led around a minute dance floor to their table. Huge windows gave a vista of a flower-filled garden and, high above, they were enclosed by a roof of sapphire blue glass. Banks of flowers hid tiny fountains which tinkled softly in the background.

It's like fairyland, thought Lacey, imagine it in winter when it's dark outside.

They were seated at a small round table. Thick wax candles made pools of flickering light around the room.

'Good. Candlelight is very flattering,' said Lacey.

'You don't need candlelight to flatter you,' said Rob. 'You would look utterly lovely in any light.'

'I wasn't asking for a compliment,' Lacey reproved him gently. 'I was simply stating a fact.'

'So was I,' he retorted, accepting a menu from the waiter.

Lacey studied her menu. 'What a

wonderful choice. I think I would like the asparagus spears with crispy bacon and mustard sauce. What do you think?'

'Sounds fine. I've never been here before, so I don't know what it would be like. I'm going to have the roast tomato and oregano soup.'

'You can have soup at any time,' said Lacey. 'I like to have something different when I go out.'

'So what will you have next? What about Saffron-poached Monkfish Loin? That sounds different.'

'You're making fun of me.'

'No. Look, it's here on the menu.'

'I'll have Duck with Wild Mushrooms. I adore duck.'

'I'm torn between Lamb and a Fillet of beef.'

'For an adventurer, you're not adventurous with food, are you?'

'Not when I'm in England. I have enough of that when I'm away.'

The wine waiter approached, and Rob ordered a Merlot for himself and a Hock for Lacey. She had never been much of a drinker and the light German wine suited her perfectly.

'So your next book is to be set in Capri. Will there be a secret perfume formula in the story?'

'No. Not that. I have to think up my own plot. Perhaps I can use that some time in the future.'

'Why didn't you tell me you were a writer?'

'You didn't ask me,' he replied, facetiously. 'I'm sorry. I didn't tell you because I wasn't a writer then. Not a published one, anyway. I didn't tell anyone. If you talk about your dreams, they often don't come true.'

'Have you always dreamed of being a writer?' she asked him genuinely.

'Since I was a child. I've always scribbled but only recently to some purpose.'

Their first course arrived and they concentrated on the food.

'Delicious.' Lacey dabbed at her lips with her napkin. 'How is your soup?'

'Excellent.' Rob replaced his spoon.

'Now tell me about the film star. Was she pleased with her perfume? I hope so after all our efforts?'

They talked at length of Claudio Capua and the perfume and Uncle Max and his perfume laboratory.

'He was shut in there for hours, day after day,' said Lacey. 'And all for one bottle of perfume.'

'Not just one — thousands, if their plans work out,' said Rob.

'And what about your plans?' asked Lacey. 'Will you stay at home now and write books?'

The waiter came to remove their plates so she had to wait for Rob's reply. He gave her a level look.

'Travelling is essential for my stories,' he said. 'I can't sit at home writing Agatha Christie style detective novels. I need to experience other countries, other cultures . . . adventures, if I can.'

Lacey nervously rubbed the tablecloth in front of her. Between them lay her outburst the last time they'd had dinner together. Rob couldn't know how she'd agonised over that incident, how she realised that she loved him for what he was. He was watching her. She felt it but she couldn't look at him.

Then with a flurry, their main course arrived. The topic was temporarily forgotten as they admired the colourful presentation of the food.

'If it tastes as good as it looks, we're in for a treat,' observed Rob.

* * *

Later, they danced. The floor was tiny; only a few couples could dance at any one time. Lacey, held closely in Rob's arms, abandoned herself to the music and the gentle movement.

'In that dress you should swoop and glide round a huge ballroom, not shuffle, in this tiny space,' he murmured in her ear.

'I'm quite happy to be squashed in this tiny space,' she answered.

He tilted his head back and looked down at her face, with his glinting blue eyes sparkling in the dim light.

'Can I take that as a compliment?'

She smiled but said nothing. His arms tightened round her.

Don't let the music stop, she prayed, silently, I want to stay like this all night.

But the music did end and they returned to their table. Rob signalled to the waiter who nodded and soon appeared with a bottle of champagne nestling in a bucket of ice.

'To your book,' Lacey raised her glass with its storm of tiny bubbles. 'May there be many more.' He nodded and smiled then raised his own glass.

'And to Lucrezia's Secret.' They drank again, laughing lightly together. 'And another toast,' he said serious again. 'To my lovely companion in adventure.'

She had a sudden feeling that he was saying goodbye. She didn't know why she thought it, but his toast sounded final. Unbidden, her eyes filled with tears.

'Lacey, what's wrong?'

'Nothing. The bubbles,' she said. 'They make my eyes water.'

'Have some more and you'll become immune to them.' He refilled their glasses. 'One more toast. 'To us'.'

'To us,' she whispered.

★ ★ ★

She was quiet on the way home. To his concerned query, she answered that she was a little sleepy.

On the doorstep, he held her hands in his against his chest and looked searchingly into her eyes.

'Thank you, Lacey, for a lovely evening.'

'I've enjoyed it so much,' she whispered back.

He slipped his arms around her and held her close for what seemed like a long time. His kiss was firm but gentle.

Her arms wound about his neck and she returned his kiss with a passion which surprised him. He made no comment, but kissed her again.

'Goodnight, my love,' he said. 'I'll see you soon.'

She opened the door, and when she had disappeared, Rob hurried back to his waiting taxi.

Lacey went quickly upstairs. It had been a wonderful, but frustrating, evening. She had secretly hoped for, but not expected, a proposal. She had expected a declaration of love.

Perhaps he was a loner, the sort of man who didn't need love. A man who would never say he loved a girl because then he would feel trapped.

Sadly, she undressed and got into bed. What would she tell Uncle Max? He had great expectations of this relationship. He saw himself as a matchmaker.

Her eyes flickered sleepily and then closed. She would deal with Uncle Max in the morning.

10

The morning brought something which occupied them both throughout breakfast. Two small pieces of cream and gold card invited them both to the wedding of Signorina Claudia Capua to Mr Charles Denier. 'How exciting,' said Lacey, 'I didn't expect this.'

'They are to be married in England,' said Uncle Max. 'I thought Italy, perhaps on the Isle of Capri.'

Lacey studied her card. 'It says, Saint Anthony's Church and a reception at Marshfield Manor. She looked at her uncle.'

'That's his place near Bath,' he said. 'Very grand, I believe. He lives there with his mother.'

'If she is very grand too, I wonder what she thinks of having an Italian film star as a daughter-in-law,' asked Lacey with a giggle.

'You'll have to go shopping again,' said Uncle Max. 'What will you buy this time?' He rather enjoyed Lacey's shopping expeditions.

'The place will be full of film stars and glamorous people. No one will notice what I wear.'

'Silly attitude.' Her uncle stood up and picking up the morning paper he had discarded when the post arrived, tucked it under his arm. 'I'm going to read this in the summer house. You've got two weeks to find something to stun everyone, young lady. I shall expect to escort the most eye-catching guest there. I don't like weddings and I don't want to travel all the way to Bath, so you'd better make it worth my while.' And with that, he marched out of the French windows and into the garden.

Lacey watched him go in amazement, then smiling to herself, went upstairs to get ready for work.

★ ★ ★

Two weeks later, dressed in the lavender blue suit and cream hat which she'd chosen for the wedding, Lacey went downstairs to wait for Uncle Max.

'I thought women were supposed to take a long time getting ready,' she muttered, glancing at the mantelpiece clock.

Uncle Max had booked a car and driver to take them to Bath. 'Might as well go in comfort,' he'd said.

The car would be outside in ten minutes. Lacey went back upstairs and stood outside Uncle Max's bedroom door. She listened, but there was no sound from inside. She tapped lightly.

'Uncle Max, are you ready? The car will be here in a few minutes.'

The door opened and her uncle came out dressed in the smoking jacket he often wore in the house.

Lacey looked at him in horror. 'But you haven't even started to get ready.'

'I'm not going,' he said, simply.

'You're not . . . But I can't go alone.'

'You won't go alone. If I'm not

191

mistaken, your escort is at the door.'

Lacey went to the banister and looked down into the hall. Mrs Wragg had admitted a tall, elegant figure in morning dress. Lacey flew down the stairs.

'Rob! Whatever is going on?'

Uncle Max had followed her down. 'I have rearranged things a little. Rob is going instead of me.'

Before Lacey could speak a word, another knock at the door announced the arrival of their car.

'Off you go.' Uncle Max shooed them towards the door. 'And bring me back your pieces of wedding cake. I love wedding cake.'

In the car, Lacey and Rob looked at each other. 'I've a feeling he's throwing us together,' smiled Rob.

Lacey flushed. 'I'm sorry.'

'I'm not. It's wonderful.' He took her hand. 'May I say you look absolutely beautiful. You'll rival the bride.'

'I hope not. That would be very bad manners.' She laughed to soften the effect of her words. 'And may I say you look very handsome.'

'I look like a tailor's dummy. But I don't mind. Anything to have a long comfortable car journey with you.' He looked round the car. 'I could get used to a life of luxury like this.'

'Well write some best sellers and you may get the chance!'

Lacey gazed out of the window at the passing countryside. She was getting used to Rob's flirtatious conversations now. He meant nothing by it. He certainly didn't mean that he loved her. He wanted them to be friends, nothing more. Very well, she would stifle her love for him and play the game too. They were just good friends, then.

★ ★ ★

An hour later, they swept up the tree-lined drive of Marshfield Manor. They gazed in awe at the beautiful old Tudor house with its golden brick and small-paned windows. There were two wings to the house, and in the centre a stone bridge crossed the moat into the courtyard.

The car followed the drive round to the right and stopped outside the church on the edge of the park land.

Rob and Lacey made their way through a crowd of happy, laughing villagers, who cheered the guests as they arrived. Lacey felt embarrassed but Rob enjoyed himself, smiling and waving.

The church was crowded already and Lacey recognised many famous faces. They were conducted to their seats and it was not long before, to the sound of the bridal march, Claudia Capua made her slow way down the aisle. There was a universal intake of breath at her ravishing dress, but Lacey and Rob were waiting for something else.

She passed them gracefully in a cloud of exquisite perfume, seductive, sensuous and rich. They looked at each other in triumph as the scent wafted around the church.

Rob leaned towards Lacey to whisper in her ear. 'I shall buy you a huge bottle of Lucrezia's Secret to wear at our wedding.'

Her head shot round and she stared at him, wide-eyed and disbelieving. Before she could whisper back, he touched a finger to his lips to silence her — the service had started.

Lacey missed most of it. She was unable to concentrate. Had he said, at our wedding or had she imagined it? He kept his face turned away from her.

While the wedding party was in the vestry, a few people slipped out to take up strategic positions with their rose petals. Rob took Lacey's hand.

'Come on. Quickly.' He led her out of the church, through the crowds and into a flower filled garden beyond. The river bank edged the garden and he guided her along its shaded walk. He stopped and took her in his arms.

She looked at him, unable to speak for emotion.

'I'm sorry I can't kneel,' he said.

'This suit is hired. I can't take it back with muddy knees.'

Lacey began to laugh. 'Oh Rob, I do love you.'

'Well, that's a start. Do you love me enough to marry me? Darling Lacey, will you marry me?'

'Of course I will. How could you ever doubt it?'

THE END

We do hope that you have enjoyed reading this large print book.

Did you know that all of our titles are available for purchase?

We publish a wide range of high quality large print books including:
Romances, Mysteries, Classics
General Fiction
Non Fiction and Westerns

Special interest titles available in large print are:
The Little Oxford Dictionary
Music Book, Song Book
Hymn Book, Service Book

Also available from us courtesy of Oxford University Press:
Young Readers' Dictionary
(large print edition)
Young Readers' Thesaurus
(large print edition)

For further information or a free brochure, please contact us at:
Ulverscroft Large Print Books Ltd.,
The Green, Bradgate Road, Anstey,
Leicester, LE7 7FU, England.
Tel: (00 44) **0116 236 4325**
Fax: (00 44) **0116 234 0205**

Other titles in the
Linford Romance Library:

ENCORE FOR A DREAM

Sheila Lewis

Limelight Theatre, struggling to survive, is temporarily saved when three sisters unexpectedly inherit it. Rosalind, Olivia and Beatrice are captivated by its charm and the loyalty of the company. With no theatrical experience, the girls strive to combine their own careers with working at Limelight — especially with Gil, the dedicated theatre director. However, an ongoing shortage of cash, a disastrous storm and unforseen tragedy threatens everyone's livelihood, while the girls also have to deal with personal emotional turmoil . . .

REAP THE WHIRLWIND

Wendy Kremer

Briana, passionate about environmental protection, is visiting Turtle Island in the Caribbean. When she discovers Phoebe, the elderly owner of the island, is considering selling it to Nick, Briana is concerned that he'd exploit the island. Determined to prevent this, she attempts to establish 'friendly tourism' there instead, although Nick is extremely sceptical. In reality he doesn't want to change a thing — but certainly relishes a fight. But when Phoebe has a heart attack, he blames Briana's new scheme . . .

IN DANGER OF LOVE

Sheila Holroyd

Ellie and the Earl of Arlbury were virtual strangers, but in a war-torn country they were forced to rely on each other to survive. Outside the normal rules of their society they developed a strong bond which drew them ever closer. But then it looked as if their luck had finally run out, the dangers that had pursued them from the start seemed to have triumphed, and they were threatened by a final, tragic parting . . .

LOVE IN THE MIST

Rosemary A. Smith

1883. Charlotte Trent has secured a post as companion to Lina, seventeen-year-old daughter of the handsome Richard Roseby, at Middlepark in Devon, and has promptly fallen in love with her employer. But not everything is quite as it seems at Middlepark . . . When Charlotte finds a bundle of old love letters hidden in her room she wonders who is Madeline? And the mysterious Anna? And what are Richard's true feelings towards the lovely, and recently widowed, Verity Hawksworth?

MOVING ON

Valerie Holmes

Hailey had prepared her younger sister, Kate, for a life at university; a brighter future than her own. But then Kate falls in love with an older man, David, suddenly leaving Hailey free. Meanwhile James, a successful, wealthy but unfulfilled PR Manager, finds his plans foiled when an accident causes him to miss his flight . . . and one kind act surprisingly leads to another . . . Both Hailey and James' lives change as they move on and in the process they discover love.